"I hope that teaches you a lesson," Tia said.

"It sure does," Tamera said.

"I'm glad to hear it," Tia said, smiling at her sister. "You mean you've finally learned that chasing after guys isn't worth it?"

"No, I've learned that if you want to impress a guy, don't wear a hair net," Tamera said.

"Tamera! You're hopeless!" Tia exclaimed. "Don't tell me you haven't given up on this crazy Barry thing? After what happened today?"

"Of course I haven't given up," Tamera said. "I'm going to get Barry to notice me or I'm going to die trying!"

**Books by Janet Quin-Harkin**

SISTER, SISTER
Cool in School
You Read My Mind
One Crazy Christmas
Homegirl on the Range
Star Quality
He's All That
Summer Daze
All Rapped Up

TGIF!
#1 Sleepover Madness
#2 Friday Night Fright
#3 Four's a Crowd
#4 Forever Friday
#5 Toe-Shoe Trouble
#6 Secret Valentine

Available from MINSTREL Books

# ALL
# RAPPED UP

## JANET QUIN-HARKIN

A
MINSTREL®
BOOK

Published by POCKET BOOKS
New York London Toronto Sydney Tokyo Singapore

This book is a work of fiction. Names, characters, places and incidents are products of the author's imagination or are used fictitiously. Any resemblance to actual events or locales or persons, living or dead, is entirely coincidental.

A MINSTREL PAPERBACK *Original*

 A Minstrel Book published by
POCKET BOOKS, a division of Simon & Schuster Inc.
1230 Avenue of the Americas, New York, NY 10020

ISBN: 0-671-00288-0

First Minstrel Books printing October 1997

10  9  8  7  6  5  4  3  2  1

A MINSTREL BOOK and colophon are registered trademarks of
Simon & Schuster Inc.

Printed in the U.S.A.

# Chapter 1

@@

*T*amera Campbell stood alone in the school hallway and let the tide of passing students wash around her. She felt like a salmon trying to swim upstream. Nobody even seemed to notice she was there, until a very large senior guy bumped into her and growled, "Hey, watch where you're going."

"Watch where *you're* going," Tamera grumbled.

Talk about the invisible woman, she said to herself. She had gone from being the star of *Romeo and Juliet* to being a nobody again, and she didn't like it one bit.

She scanned the passing faces, hoping to catch a glimpse of her twin sister, Tia Landry. She hadn't seen her since they'd gotten off the bus that morning and Tia had headed for the library. Over the past year Tamera had gotten used to having Tia beside her all the time. She liked the security of looking across at Tia and whispering, "What's an ecosystem?" or, more often, "What page are we on?" Now Tia's classes had all been switched around, and Tamera was feeling lost.

At last she saw the familiar brown beret. Tamera fought her way through the crowd and grabbed her sister just before she disappeared.

"Tia, wait a second," she said panting.

"Oh, hi, Tamera," Tia said. "What's up?"

"Nothing's up. It's just that I never get to see you these days," Tamera said. "I'm feeling abandoned. Today in English the teacher called on me to read and—"

"Let me guess—you didn't know where you were supposed to start."

"Worse than that. I didn't know what book we were in!"

"Tamera! You've got to wise up sometime, you know," Tia said, laughing. "Only two more years and then college. That's going to be way harder."

"Don't worry about me," Tamera said. "I'm going to major in a subject that I really like."

"Such as?"

Tamera shrugged. "It's a tough choice," she said.

"I'm impressed," Tia said. "I thought you didn't really like any of your classes that much."

"I don't," Tamera said. "The choice is between TV sitcoms, shopping, and boys. If you hear about any colleges that offer those majors, let me know, will you?"

Tia gave her sister a shove. "Tamera, you're hopeless," she said.

"But fun, huh?" Tamera said. "I bet I'm more fun than those boring people in your new honors classes."

Tia made a face. "I'd have to agree with you there," she said. "I'm with a lot of supersmart people, but they take everything so seriously. I asked the girl next to me if she'd heard REM, and she said you didn't hear rapid eye movements, you observed them during sleep. She'd never even heard of the rock group!"

"What a dork!" Tamera said. It felt good to be laughing with Tia again. "Are you coming to the concert today?" she asked.

"Concert? What concert?"

"You know—the Wednesday talent show in the gym. I hear there's a good group performing today."

"I don't know, Tamera," Tia said. "I've got some stuff to finish in the library."

"Forget the library for once," Tamera said. "Think of your poor sister, sitting all alone with no one to talk to at lunch."

"You've got Marcia and Denise and the rest of the gang." Tia laughed.

"Yeah, but it's not the same without you," Tamera said. She noticed Tia looking around nervously.

"I know Miss Perfect here doesn't want to be late to class," Tamera added. "Which way are you heading?"

"I've got math right now," Tia said, and she made a face. "I'm heading to room five-oh-one, and it's beginning to feel like the Five-oh-one Blues."

"I thought you loved math," Tamera said.

"I do," Tia answered. "It's just that I'm not too crazy about my new teacher. I know I've only been there a few days, but I get the feeling he doesn't like me."

"Who couldn't like you?" Tamera demanded. "You're just like me and everyone adores *me*." Then her smile faded. "Seriously, Tia. What is there not to like about you? You have to be the world's most perfect student."

"I know," Tia said, grinning, "but I'm still getting bad vibes from the teacher. Maybe he doesn't like students being moved around in the middle of the school year, but he wasn't exactly welcoming when I came into the class last week."

"Then I'll remind myself not to do so well that

I get promoted to the honors class," Tamera said. "I like Ms. Morgenstern."

"Me, too," Tia said. "I thought she was the best teacher. I'm beginning to think that she was the only reason I was doing well in math."

"Don't be silly," Tamera said. "You were doing well because you're supersmart."

"I used to think I was smart," Tia said, "but this new guy makes me so nervous that I can't think straight. The very first day he called me up to do a problem on the board, my mind went blank. I felt like an idiot.

"You get used to it," Tamera said. "I feel that way every time a teacher calls on me. Except in math. I've got math down pat." She smiled mysteriously. "Did you see that A I got on my last homework?" she added smugly. "Ms. Morgenstern was very impressed."

"You—an A in math? You're sure you're the same twin sister I've always had and not a new clone of me?"

Tamera was still smiling mysteriously. "I've just been putting my talents to full use," she said. "I decided what I did best, and I've been doing it, and it's been working just fine."

"Tamera, that's great," Tia said. "Your dad is going to be so happy. Remember how excited he was that time we switched places and he thought you were getting A's in math? Too bad you don't have a boyfriend right now. Your dad would probably let you stay out as late as you wanted on school nights if you were doing great in school."

"Yeah, right," Tamera said gloomily. "All the time in the world and no one special to share it with."

"You'll find another boyfriend soon," Tia said. "We both will."

"I hope so," Tamera said. "The spring formal is coming up. I really want to go."

"Then go."

"Slight problem—I need someone to dance *with!*" Tamera said. She stopped in front of a big, glittery poster. "Dancing in the Dark," it said in silver glitter letters on black paper. "Annual Spring Formal. Tickets go on sale next week in office. $10 per person."

"I have to go to this dance, Tia," Tamera said. "Now all I need is the right guy to go with."

"Did I hear someone calling my name?" a voice asked behind them.

The girls spun around.

"Roger! What are you doing here?" Tamera demanded, glaring at her pint-size neighbor, who always managed to bug her.

"I was just walking through the halls when I saw a damsel in distress," Roger said, beaming at her. "I thought I heard a certain girl say that she'd love to go to the dance and all she needed was the right guy to escort her. Well, here I am—ready, willing, and able to offer my services."

"Roger, get real," Tamera said, wrinkling her nose. "I wouldn't go with you if you were the last guy in the city of Detroit."

She started to move away. Roger stood in the middle of the hall, gazing at her adoringly. "Okay, so I'll move to Australia," he called after her. "Then would you go with me?"

"Uggghhhh!" Tamera growled as she and Tia turned the corner. "Doesn't he ever give up?"

"I think it's cute," Tia said. "I really admire that kind of devotion in a guy. His love for you is stronger than your hatred of him. Nothing discourages him or makes him stray from his quest."

Tia jumped as she felt a tap on her shoulder. It was Roger again.

"Tia?" he said, beaming at her. "I've got a question to ask you. If Tamera won't go to the dance with me, how about you and me going instead?"

"Are you out of your mind? Never in a million years, you little creep," Tia said, and strode on down the hall.

Tamera was laughing as she ran to catch up with her sister. "Nothing can make him stray from his quest?"

"You be quiet," Tia snapped.

"At least we don't have to worry about the dance now," Tamera went on. "We know that, in a worst-case scenario, we always have Roger to escort us."

"That really would be the worst case, Tamera," Tia said. "I'm just hoping we come up with something better between now and then."

"Me, too," Tamera said.

The bell rang, and students started to drift toward their classrooms.

"Tamera, I don't want to make you late for your own class," Tia said. "You don't have to walk me all the way to math."

"That's okay," Tamera said. "The teacher would have a fit if I was on time. Besides, I'm hoping to bump into somebody who has a locker in this hall."

"Who?" Tia asked.

Tamera tossed her hair. "You wouldn't know him."

"It's a he?"

"Just a guy from my math class," Tamera said.

"I knew you couldn't survive without a guy in your life for long."

Tamera held up her hand. "It's not like that at all," she said. "We're just friends. We share intellectual interests."

"Huh!" Tia said. "I'll believe that when I see it."

Tamera stiffened. "Oh, here he comes now," she said. "Okay, 'bye, Tia. See you at lunch. Meet you in the gym. Don't forget."

"Are you crazy?" Tia asked. "You don't think I'm going to leave now without getting a good look at this new guy."

"I told you, it's not like that. Charles isn't exactly my idea of a hunk. So you can go to your math class and leave us alone to talk."

She pushed past Tia and caught up with a tall, lanky boy dressed in a preppy-style button-down shirt and V-neck sweater. Tia watched with interest and saw the boy's face light up as Tamera walked over to him.

The hallway was emptying out so Tia was able to watch as the boy opened his backpack and took out a sheet of paper. Now she was very curious. Tamera had seemed anxious to get rid of her when she'd spotted this guy. And there was something about the way she took the paper from him that looked sneaky. What was there about a sheet of paper that Tamera didn't want Tia to see?

Tamera took the paper and stuffed it into a book she was carrying. "Thanks a million, Charles," she said.

"No problem, Tamera," Charles said as he headed down the hall.

"What was that all about?" Tia asked as she ran to catch up with her sister.

"Nothing," Tamera said. "Just some stuff he was copying out for me."

"Than why did it look like I was watching an old spy movie," Tia said.

"You'd better get to your math class. You're going to be late."

"Tamera?" Tia insisted.

At that moment Charles turned around and walked back toward them. "I'm sorry, I meant to tell you, Tamera. I'm going to be away with my parents all weekend, so if you've got any homework you need done, I'll have to have it by Thursday," he said. Then with a wave he headed off down the hall.

# Chapter 2

#### ෨

"Okay, do you mind telling me what that was all about?" Tia demanded. "Homework you need *done*? Tamera, is that guy doing your homework?"

"Only my math homework," Tamera said defensively. "And he volunteered to do it. He just moved here, and he developed an instant crush on me—which shows he'd got good taste. I told him I was having problems with math, and he offered to help me."

"But that's not helping," Tia said angrily. "That's cheating, Tamera."

"No, it's helping. It's helping me get an A in math. What could be more helpful than that?"

"Doing it yourself would be more helpful. You'll

only understand the subject matter by doing your own work."

"I wasn't understanding it when I *was* doing my own work," Tamera said. "The way I see it, it's a whole lot better to get an A and not understand the work than to get an F and not understand."

"You're hopeless," Tia said. "And you're using him."

"I am not," Tamera said. "If you really want to know, it makes Charles happy to think that he's doing something for me. I just love bringing happiness into the world."

Tia rolled her eyes. "Gotta run," she said, then darted into the math classroom just as Mr. Wilson, the math teacher, began to close the door.

"Almost late again, Ms. Landry?" he said. "What was it this time—powdering your nose or fixing your hair?"

"Excuse me?" Tia asked. She wasn't sure she had heard right.

"Isn't that what young women spend all their time doing—when they're not gossiping on the phone?"

"Not this young woman," Tia said. "I have never powdered my nose in my life."

She strode to her seat and glared at the grinning boy next to her. "What's so funny, Jonathan?" she demanded.

"Nothing." Jonathan looked down hurriedly at his math book.

Tia opened her books and sat there, pencil at the ready.

Mr. Wilson walked across to the blackboard. "Okay, guys—or should I say guys and gals?" he asked with a raised eyebrow.

Tia looked around the classroom and noticed something that hadn't struck her until now. There were very few girls in the class.

"Let's get started on those proofs that were giving us trouble yesterday." Mr. Wilson started sketching a complicated geometric figure on the board. "Now," he said, "I seem to remember we were having trouble finding the area of this small piece. Let's call it the garage, shall we? Or, for the benefit of the ladies present, should we say the shoe store at the shopping mall?"

Tia opened her eyes wide and looked up. Mr. Wilson was still standing there, smiling and looking like a kindly grandfather. And yet she couldn't have misunderstood twice. She saw Joanie Chen glance across at her and make a face.

"Okay, so any suggestions on a way to tackle this?" Mr. Wilson asked, looking around the classroom.

Tia looked at the figure on the board, then raised her hand. Mr. Wilson's gaze swept over her as if she were invisible. "Anybody?" he asked. "What about you, Frank?"

A boy in the front row mumbled something.

"Not quite, but you're on the right track," Mr. Wilson said. "How about you, Marcus? Ramon?" Then finally he seemed to notice Tia's waving hand. "Oh well, guys, I can see there's a little lady just dying to show you up. Go ahead, Ms. Landry."

Tia was feeling hot and embarrassed as she got to her feet. She found herself stumbling over words, which was something she never did. But she was determined to show this annoying man that she could do the problem. When she finished, she sat down again. For a moment there was silence, then Mr. Wilson said, "You seem to have hit on the right solution, Ms. Landry. Or was that just a lucky guess?"

"It was the right solution, using the proof that you taught us at the beginning of the week," Tia said coldly.

"Okay, keep your hair on," Mr. Wilson said. "Guys who have been in my class before will tell you that I like to kid around, just like I used to when I was the football coach—right, guys?"

A few boys nodded.

"So if you can't take the kidding, then go back to Ms. Morgenstern. I understand she's very gentle with you girls."

Mr. Wilson went on with the lesson. Tia was

feeling so angry that she was about to explode. She had never, in her whole life, come up against a teacher who put her down, and that was just what Mr. Wilson doing. She thought about going to the principal, but she didn't want to do that just yet. She knew how tough it was to get into the honors class. If she complained during her first week in the class. Mr. Wilson would tell the principal that she couldn't handle the class and would be better off back with Ms. Morgenstern. Tia got the feeling that was exactly what he wanted to happen.

She didn't raise her hand to answer a question again, but she spent the time trying to work out what to say to Mr. Wilson. Obviously they had gotten off on the wrong foot for some reason. She had to find out what made him not like her and change that before it was too late. If she talked to him one-on-one and told him how uncomfortable he was making her feel, she was sure they could work things out.

When the bell rang, Tia lingered at Mr. Wilson's desk.

"Anything wrong, Ms. Landry?" he asked. "Was there something you didn't understand and were afraid to ask in front of all the boys?"

"No," Tia said firmly. "I understood everything just fine, except for one thing."

"And that was?"

"For some reason I get the feeling that you don't

want me in this class," Tia blurted out. She hadn't meant to say it that way, but her anger was spilling over.

"I didn't have any choice in the matter," Mr. Wilson said, pretending to examine a pile of papers on his desk.

"But if you did have a choice, you'd rather teach all boys?" Tia demanded. "You think girls don't belong in advanced math?"

"I didn't say that," Mr. Wilson said slowly. "But when you think about it, what usually happens to girls? They push hard to get ahead, and then they go get married and waste all that education."

Tia blinked again. "Mr. Wilson, first of all, boys get married, too. And for your information, I intend to go to college and make something of my life. I might be a doctor, I might be an engineer, but whatever I choose, you'd better believe I'm going to be good at it!"

"That's what they all say at your age," Mr. Wilson said.

"I don't believe you're saying this," Tia said.

"It's just the way I am," Mr. Wilson said. "If you don't like it, then you can always transfer back to your old class."

"You're not getting rid of me so easily," Tia said. "I'm staying in this class, and what's more, I'm getting an A!"

Then she stormed out of the room. Once she

was in the empty hallway, she wondered what to do next. Part of her wanted to go tell the principal the whole conversation, but she knew Mr. Vernon probably wouldn't be in his office during lunch hour. He liked to wander around the campus and catch students smoking or trying to sneak out.

Sneaking out was exactly what Tia felt like doing at that moment. She wanted to walk and walk, feeling the wind in her hair, until she had blown away the bad taste that was in her mouth. Tia could never remember feeling so angry before. She was being judged and put down, just because she was a girl, and it wasn't fair!

She rounded the corner and strode down the back hall, wanting to get to the fresh air as quickly as possible when a door opened and she was hit with a blast of sound. For a moment she stood there, confused. Then she remembered—the Wednesday talent show. She was supposed to be meeting Tamera in the gym.

Reluctantly she opened the gym door and went inside. A rock group was still playing and the whole gym throbbed with sound. Tia wished she was anywhere but here right now. She wasn't in the mood to be anything but angry.

Tia had almost convinced herself that Tamera wouldn't care if she was there or not and was about to slip out the door when she saw Tamera waving to her from the top of the bleachers. Tia took a deep breath then clambered up through the crowd to join her sister.

"Great group, huh?" Tamera asked as Tia slipped onto the bench beside her. "And you're lucky. You didn't miss the rappers. They're just about to go on."

Tia was about to tell Tamera about her horrible encounter with Mr. Wilson, but her first words were drowned out by yells and applause as three boys walked to the center of the gym floor. They were wearing black and white striped long-sleeved shirts, red suspenders holding up black baggy pants, and black baseball caps worn backward. One sat at the drums, one at a turntable, and the other one grabbed a mike from its stand. The beat started and they launched into their rap.

" 'Gonna tell you 'bout a guy who thought he was cool,/And didn't have nothin' to learn in school,' " they began.

It was a funny song about a guy who drops out and what happened to him. Tia was only half listening, but she could hear the laughter all around her. The lead rapper was someone Tia had seen around school. He was tall and very good-looking in a lean, angular sort of way. The way he moved told everyone he knew he was Mr. Cool. Tia didn't like people who acted like that, so arrogant, even though she had to admit he was good as he performed the rap.

When the number was over, the audience went wild, screaming and stomping their feet. All around Tia and Tamera the bleachers were emptying. At last Tia stood up. "Ready to go?" she asked her sister. "I don't know about you, but I'm starving. Tamera, you'll never believe what just happened to me. Remember I told you about Mr. Wilson, the math teacher, and how he doesn't like me?"

She looked down at her sister. Tamera was still staring out across the gym as if she were in a trance.

"Earth to Tamera," Tia said, jerking her to her feet. "Are you okay?"

"I'm fine, just fine," Tamera said. "In fact, I've never felt better in my whole life. I've just found the guy I'm going to the spring formal with."

"You have? Who?"

"Him!" Tamera said, pointing to the lead singer of the rap group, who was now surrounded by adoring girls and clearly enjoying every minute of it.

Tia laughed. "You're crazy, Tamera. You don't even know him."

"No, but I intend to," Tamera said with a happy sigh. "I know his name. Barry. Nice, huh? Barry and Tamera."

"Nothing personal, Tamera," Tia said, "but I

think it looks like you've got a little competition there."

Tamera looked at the girls who were still fighting for Barry's attention. "I thrive on competition," she said.

"You're not exactly in his league," Tia added.

"I don't see why not," Tamera said. "He's a student here and so am I, and I'm good-looking and so is he."

"Dream on, girl" Tia said.

"You just wait," Tamera said. "He is definitely the coolest guy I've ever seen, and I'm going to make him notice me or die trying."

Barry was now crossing the floor, carrying a mike stand. He stopped to call out to someone in the bleachers below the twins. His eyes sparkled and he smiled, showing the most perfect white teeth Tamera had ever seen. He finished what he was saying with a little impromptu dance step.

Tamera sighed. "Isn't he gorgeous, Tia? Wasn't his rap funny? And the way he moves—imagine him on the dance floor with me. Everyone would notice us."

"And just how do you plan to meet this guy and get him to ask you to the dance, all in three short weeks?" Tia demanded.

"I'll come up with something," Tamera said. "I've dazzled quite a few guys with my charm and personality."

"Tamera, you've dazzled Roger. That's about it."

"Hey, that's not fair, and it's not even true. What about Lamar? You have to admit he was cute!"

"Yes, but you got to know each other when you rehearsed for the play together. That's different."

"I'll find a way to get Barry to notice me," Tamera said.

"He's standing down there all alone. Go speak to him right now," Tia said.

Tamera shot her sister a horrified look. "Are you crazy? These things take time and lots of preparation," she said. "I can't just *go over* to him. I have to look right, be in the right place at the right time, and make him realize that I am the only girl in the world for him. Right now I look totally blah. In fact, let's get out of here before he notices me."

She hurried down from the bleachers ahead of Tia and out of the gym.

# Chapter 3

❧

*T*ia couldn't stop thinking about Mr. Wilson all afternoon. The moment school was out, she got up her courage and went to the principal's office. Principal Vernon smiled at her warmly.

"Tia, good to see you. Entering any more science fairs?"

Tia stood in front of his desk. "Mr. Vernon," she said. "I've got a problem."

"What is it?"

"It's Mr. Wilson," she blurted out. "He's giving me a hard time in honors math. He told me today that it was a waste of time educating girls because they only got married."

To her surprise Principal Vernon smiled. "Don't

let him upset you, Tia. He likes to challenge his students."

"A challenge is one thing, but this is too much. Teachers shouldn't be allowed to say things like that," Tia exploded. "How many girls do you think he's discouraged during the time he's been teaching?"

Principal Vernon nodded. "I hear what you're saying, Tia," he said, "but since I wasn't there I can't make a judgment on it. It sounds like he was teasing you and you overreacted. Besides," he added, "he's the only one who is qualified to teach the advanced classes and, quite frankly, he's a good teacher."

"How can he be a good teacher if he doesn't want to teach half the students?" Tia demanded.

"Don't worry, I'm sure he'll back down when he sees that you are a serious student," Principal Vernon said. "Just let him see that he doesn't scare you and you'll be fine."

"You mean I've got to sit there and take his stupid jokes and put-downs?"

"It's good training for life, Tia. You're going to come up against men who don't think that women belong in business, in medicine, or other fields, and you're going to have to learn to handle them."

He got up from his chair. "I'll have a word with Mr. Wilson and warn him that I expect him to treat all his students equally. In the meantime, I want you to hang in there and rise to the challenge.

And, I want you to know that you have my full support, Tia."

"Thanks," Tia said, hoping she was hiding the bitterness she felt. "Thanks for nothing," she muttered under her breath as she walked out of the office.

She couldn't wait to get home and tell her mother about everything that had happened. At least she knew that Lisa would understand. Tia had tried telling Tamera after they had left the gym, but Tamera's mind was only on Barry and didn't seem to think it was a big deal anyway. "Then go back to Ms. Morgenstern," she had said. "You know she's a nice person."

"But she doesn't teach advanced math," Tia had snapped.

"So? You can do advanced math in college if you want," Tamera had said.

Tamera just didn't understand how important it was to Tia. The best colleges expected applicants to take honors classes in high school. Tia knew that her sister would do anything she could to get out of taking any math classes and she would certainly never choose to take a harder class.

Tia knew her mother would understand. Lisa had had to struggle hard as a single mom. And she was a fighter—she had never let anyone put her down! Maybe she'd help Tia come up with the right way to handle Mr. Wilson.

Tia let herself into the house. "Hi, I'm home," she called.

Nobody answered.

"Mom? Tamera? Ray?" She ran up to the bedroom she had shared with her sister since she and her mother moved in with Tamera and Ray. Tamera wasn't there. The house was empty.

Tia threw down her book bag and tried to get started on her homework, but she was too worked up to concentrate. Every time she started on a math problem, she imagined what Mr. Wilson would say if she messed up.

Tia closed her math book and went to the kitchen to fix herself a snack. Usually Tamera was the one who liked junk food, but today Tia had a deep craving for a sundae. She found a brownie, then she topped it with ice cream and caramel sauce, and sprinkled it with M&M's. She was just carrying it to the sofa to eat when the front door burst open and her mother, Lisa Landry, came in.

"Ooh, look at that. Comfort food. How sweet of my baby to make it for her mama. Just what I need right now," she said, taking the sundae away from the surprised Tia.

Tia reached for the dish just as the first spoonful was heading for Lisa's mouth. "Mom!" she cried. "I made this for myself."

"But you *never* eat junk food in the afternoon," Lisa said. "And I need it. And I mean *need* it. I have just had the worst time with the most obnoxious man in the world!" She slumped on the sofa and started spooning the ice cream into her mouth. "You just won't believe what I'm going to tell you, Tia," she said between mouthfuls. "I thought that kind of attitude went out with the Dark Ages. The way that man talked to me!"

"Mom, that is so weird, because the same thing happened to me today," Tia said.

"It did?"

"Yeah, my new math teacher basically told me it wasn't worth teaching girls advanced math."

"He did?" Lisa was hardly paying attention. "Well, listen to what Mr. Rojas said to me."

"Wait—who's Mr. Rojas?"

"He's the new manager of the shopping mall. He wants to raise my rent."

"The rent on your fashion cart?" Tia asked.

Lisa nodded. "I told him I thought I was already paying too much for a crummy space between the video games and the food court."

"And what did he say?"

"He said that maybe we could arrange something, *if* I went on a date with him."

"Mom! That's gross."

"You better believe it. I told him there was no way I'd date an overweight fish-faced creep like him, and then he got nasty. He said I was lowering the tone of the mall with my tacky fashion cart and he'd have me out of there one way or another!

And I said, 'Oh yeah?' and he said that no woman was a match for him."

"That's terrible," Tia said. "What makes men think that they rule the universe?"

"I don't know, but I've decided I'm through with men. From now on I'm going to devote myself to my career and my talented daughter."

"You know, you're right about guys, Mom," Tia said. "Mr. Wilson is just the same."

"Who's Mr. Wilson?"

"I was trying to tell you, but you were so mad at Mr. Rojas that you didn't listen. He's my math teacher. He treats me like I'm a joke."

"He did? Well, let me go down there and show him that my fist isn't joking when it connects with his chin."

"Mom, that wouldn't help. I just don't understand guys. They always think they're so hot, but who needs them? I'm with you. I'm giving up guys from now on."

The front door opened, and Ray Campbell, Tamera's father, walked in. "Hi, girls," he said. "Had a good day?"

Lisa glared at him. "For one thing, I'm a woman, not a girl, and for another I have had a terrible day, thanks to you."

"Me?" Ray looked puzzled. "What have I done?"

"You go around thinking that you're superior to me, acting like you're so hot."

"I most certainly do not!" Ray said, stepping back in alarm. "When have I ever done that?"

"You're a man, and all men act that way," Lisa said. "Tia and I have had it up to here with men. No more men in our lives, right, Tia?"

"Right, Mom."

"Well, I'm sorry to hear that. I guess you won't be wanting that ride to the supermarket you asked for."

"I didn't say I was giving up *using* men," Lisa said. "I can't carry home five bags of groceries by myself."

Ray chuckled as he walked into the kitchen. "So I guess you've had a bad encounter with a man today, huh?"

"Both of us," Tia said. "The manager at the mall wants to raise Mom's rent and then had the nerve to ask her on a date, and my new math teacher told me I didn't belong in his class because I was going to get married someday!"

"So two bad apples are spoiling the whole barrel for you?" Ray asked. "Not all men treat women like that, you know."

"Yeah, well, I've had more than my share lately," Lisa said. "What about that Michael guy, who thought that Tia won third prize in the science fair only because she was a girl? And what about that Tex creep who wanted me to wear an apron and do what he told me? That's enough for me, buster. No more men in my life."

"Me neither," Tia said. "I'm with you, Mom, all the way."

The front door burst open, and Tamera made a grand entrance. "Isn't it a beautiful day?" she asked, flinging her arms open wide. "Isn't the world a wonderful place?"

"What's with her?" Lisa muttered to Tia. "Is she coming down with something?"

"Sorry I'm late, but I was out doing research," Tamera went on, waltzing around the room.

"Doing research, you?" Ray asked. "My, I really am impressed, Tamera. First you start getting good grades in math, and now you're doing research. You've finally turned over a new leaf. What subject are you researching?"

"Barry Blackwell," Tamera said.

"I'm not familiar with that name," Ray said. "Is he an American poet?"

"Sort of," Tamera said.

"He's a guy at our school," Tia said dryly. "Tamera's got a crush on him. He's in a rap group."

Ray frowned. "You know what I think about rap, Tamera. I don't like the language they use, and I don't like the negative messages their music is sending out to young people. It's all about violence and destruction."

"Barry's not like that at all, Daddy," Tamera said quickly. "He did a really funny rap today. Tell him, Tia. No gangs or violence in it."

Tia nodded. "It *was* funny," she said. "And it had a positive message about staying in school."

Ray was still frowning. "I have to drive these rap singers around in my limos sometimes, and quite frankly, I don't like what I see. Too much stuff goes on at these dance clubs where they perform. They're not the kind of places I'd ever want you to go, Tamera."

"Dad, Barry goes to my school. He just performed with his group at lunch," Tamera said before Ray could forbid her to think about Barry anymore. "He's just a regular teenager who has a rap group as a hobby, that's all."

Ray smiled. "I guess that's different then."

"And it's not like Tamera is dating him or anything," Tia said, giving Tamera a look.

"But I will be," Tamera said. "I've come up with the most perfect plan."

Then she danced up the stairs, singing to herself.

Tia's curiosity got the better of her. She got up and followed Tamera up to their room.

"Okay," she said, closing the door behind her. "What is this perfect plan you've come up with? You're going to kidnap Barry and hold him hostage until he agrees to go to the dance with you? Or maybe you're going to offer him a million dollars?"

"Much simpler than that," Tamera said. "I did my research, remember. I waited around after school, and I watched him go to his car, and I've found out all about him."

"And?"

"He drives a red Mustang—cool, huh? That's the good news. The bad news is that a girl drove away with him."

"What girl?"

Tamera wrinkled her nose. "You know that girl called Whitney—the one who wears the square clompy shoes with the four-inch heels and has that gorgeous braided hair?"

"The one who's a model and whose picture is on billboards? She's his girlfriend? I told you you were wasting your time, Tamera."

"I don't see why," Tamera said. "What's she got that I don't?"

"Besides being gorgeous, talented, and having fantastic hair and the most fashionable clothes in the school? Not much," Tia said.

"Ah, but what you don't know is that I have a secret weapon," Tamera said smugly.

"Go on, surprise me."

"Your brain."

"Excuse me? What do you plan to do with my brain—sell it to a museum for megabucks and then buy a new wardrobe?"

"No, dummy. Your great brain is going to come up with a way for me to meet Barry and get him to ask me to the dance, all in three weeks!"

# Chapter 4

❧

*T*ia's eyes opened wide with amazement. "Let me get this straight," she said. "You want me to make a gorgeous, popular guy forget about his equally gorgeous girlfriend in three weeks?"

"Sure," Tamera said. "It should be no problem for someone who's in advanced math."

"I don't think they've written an equation for that one," Tia said. "And maybe my brain doesn't have time to do anything more than my homework assignments. And maybe I wouldn't want to help you if I could."

"Not want to help me? But I'm your favorite sister."

"You're my only sister."

"Exactly, so I have to be your favorite," Tamera said. "And I know you'd want me to be happy. Going to the dance with Barry would make me the happiest person in the world."

"Tamera, you don't even know this guy," Tia said. "He might be the world's biggest jerk."

"Whitney doesn't think so, and you admit that she has good taste," Tamera said. "Besides, he looks so cool, who cares if he's a jerk?"

"Tamera, when will you learn?" Tia said, shaking her head. "There are more important things in life than finding yourself the perfect guy."

"Yeah, like what?"

"Look at me," Tia said. "I'm happy and I've given up guys totally."

"You've given up guys? Since when?"

"Since I decided that all guys were chauvinist creeps. We don't need them, Tamera. We should be happy to be ourselves, enjoying each other's company—"

"Great!" Tamera walked over to the window. "My sister's finally flipped," she called to the world outside. "I knew too much studying wasn't good for her. Now her brain has finally exploded!"

"I haven't flipped, Tamera. I've just woken up and smelled the coffee," Tia said. "Mr. Wilson made me see that deep down, all guys think they're better than girls. Look at the way your dreamboat

Barry was strutting around as if he was something special."

"He is," Tamera said. "And I don't care what you say. I want to meet him more than anything in the world. And I need your help, Tia. Please?"

"How do you think I could help you?" Tia said. "It's not like he's in any of my classes."

"You could come up with clever ways for me to meet him so that it doesn't look as if I'm following him around. And then you could tell me witty, brilliant things to say to him when I've met him."

"From what I saw today I don't think he's the kind of guy who would appreciate witty or brilliant. Try adoring, Tamera. That seemed to work great with him."

"I'd be happy to be adoring, if I could find the right time and place to adore him. How come we never see him in the halls around school? I don't even know what classes he takes."

"Well I guess you could start off by going to the guidance office and looking up his schedule."

"Brilliant! How can I do that?"

"Oh, I don't know. Say you found a paper he wrote lying in the parking lot and you're sure it's important so you'd like to return it to him right away."

"Oh, that's *good*," Tamera said, her face lighting up. "You think fast."

"It's all that advanced math, I guess" Tia said with a chuckle.

"Great. Now we're getting somewhere," Tamera said. "I find out his schedule and then . . . and then . . ." Her face lit up again. "And then I change my schedule so that we have the same classes!" A worried look came over her face. "Unless he's a senior in all advanced classes. They wouldn't let me switch to honors calculus and physics, would they?"

"Tamera, they wouldn't let you into any senior classes," Tia said.

"He has to take some electives, doesn't he?" Tamera demanded. "And electives are open to anybody."

"Not in the middle of the school year," Tia said. "I can't see them letting you switch schedules in the middle of the semester without a very good reason."

"This is a very good reason."

"Yeah, but not to guidance counselors."

"I'll think of something," Tamera said. "I'm going to be like the U.S. mail. Neither rain nor hail nor sleet nor snow is going to stop Tamera Campbell in her quest."

"I don't think Barry is taking meteorology," Tia said with a grin.

"Go ahead, laugh," Tamera said. "You'll be the

one who's dying of envy when I'm dancing with Barry in three weeks."

"I won't, because I won't be there," Tia said.

Now Tamera looked worried. "You are seriously not coming to the spring formal? Tia, everyone who matters goes to the spring formal."

"Not me," Tia said. "I'll probably be at a coffee-house, having interesting discussions with my friends from the Future Female Scientists club."

"Yuck," Tamera said. "How come we've got all the same genes and mine turned out normal and yours turned out weird?" A big smile spread across her face. "I've got a great idea. Since you're not in-terested in boys anymore, how about we go through your closet and you give me all your cool clothes?"

"Dream on," Tia said. "Just because I've given up men doesn't mean I've given up looking good. Now they can all notice me and realize what they're missing out on."

Tamera opened the closet door and started going through her own clothes. "I wonder if my dad would drive me to the mall," she said. "I've got nothing in this whole closet that can compete with Whitney. If I want Barry to notice me, I've got to look good, and I mean good!"

Lisa poked her head around the bedroom door. "Did I hear somebody say she wanted to look good?" she asked.

"Yeah, but I've got no money," Tamera said.

"I know," Lisa said. "I'll bring you one of my designs from my fashion cart. You can wear that to school and dazzle everybody."

Tamera tried to give her a grateful smile. "Oh, that would dazzle everybody all right," she said.

The moment Lisa went out again, she made a horrified face to Tia. "You've got to help me," she whispered. "I can't wear one of your mom's dresses to school. Barry would think I was a creature from Mars."

She glared at Tia, who was lying on her bed laughing. "It's not funny," she said. "I mean, can you imagine me walking around school in a dress in green and orange spandex with sequins and bows all over it?"

She began to laugh, too. She threw herself down on her bed, and the twins lay there laughing. "Oh, Tia," Tamera gasped. "Why does life have to be so complicated?"

The next morning Tamera got to school early and went to the office. The only person working was the school secretary, a friendly older woman called Mrs. Green.

"I . . . uh . . . need to know somebody's schedule," Tamera said.

The secretary went across to her computer. "Whose schedule do you need, honey?" she asked.

This was easier than Tamera had imagined. "Uh . . . Barry Blackwell's?"

Mrs. Green looked at Tamera suspiciously. "What do you need it for, Tamera?"

"I . . . I found a paper he must have dropped in the parking lot. I thought he might need to turn it in right away and he'd get in trouble if it was late, so I thought I'd take it to him."

Mrs. Green smiled. "That's very thoughtful of you, Tamera. I tell you what. Why don't you give it to me and I'll see it gets to the right teacher so that it's not late."

"No! That wouldn't work at all," Tamera blurted out. "I mean, we don't know if he'd want the teacher to see it yet, do we? What if he hadn't checked it yet? I wouldn't want him to get a bad grade, would I?"

Mrs. Green was still smiling. "I only wish that Barry's as diligent as you seem to think he is," she said, "but I don't think there would be too much harm in giving you his schedule."

She called up the computer screen then made a few notes on a piece of paper. "Here you go, dear," she said. "And good luck. You're the fifth or sixth girl who has come in here asking about Barry. He must be one popular young man."

Tamera managed a weak smile as she went out. Let people laugh all they wanted. She didn't care.

Other girls might try to meet Barry, but she was the only one who was going to win!

As soon as she went into her history class, Tamera sat down and studied what Mrs. Green had written: P.E., remedial English, U.S. history, intro to algebra, auto shop, and band. She could hardly switch to intro to algebra when she was already in algebra 2. She couldn't persuade anyone that she needed remedial English when she was getting a B in regular English. And she couldn't take U.S. history. That class was for juniors and seniors. She couldn't do P.E. first period because she had her own history class then. That left auto shop and band.

Great interactive classes, Tamera said to herself. And they would work with my schedule, too. I could say I'm having trouble with science, which is definitely true, and I'm going to try it again next year. And I could switch to band instead of art. Perfect!

She closed her eyes and imagined herself working on a car with Barry. They'd be under the hood together and he'd ask her for a wrench. When she passed it to him, their hands would touch and he'd look up into her eyes. "That was just the wrench I needed, Tamera," he'd say. "How did you know that?"

"I have this feeling for cars," Tamera would say.

"My dad works with cars and I guess it's rubbed off."

"You're incredible," Barry would say. "Most girls hate getting dirty or breaking their nails."

"Not me," Tamera would say. "I just love all cars, especially Mustangs."

"What an incredible coincidence," Barry would say, "because I just happen to have—"

"Tamera?" She jumped when she heard her name.

"What?"

She noticed that the classroom was very quiet and the teacher was staring at her. She glanced hopefully at Tia.

"Columbus," Tia mouthed.

"Uh—Columbus, Ohio?" Tamera said.

There were giggles all around her. Mr. Berry, the history teacher, was frowning. "You weren't paying attention again, were you?" he asked.

Tamera decided it was better, for once, to tell the truth. "I'm sorry, Mr. Berry. I've got a big problem on my mind right now. I think I might have to change my schedule. It's worrying me."

"You might wind up with an even bigger problem if you flunk history and have to repeat it in summer school," Mr. Berry said.

Tamera opened her book and tried hard to concentrate. There was no way she wanted to find herself in summer school.

At lunch she went to see her counselor. "I want to change my schedule," she said.

Ms. Allen looked concerned. "Are you having problems with your classes, Tamera?"

Tamera nodded. "Yeah, science," she said. "I thought it might be wiser to drop it now and then take it again next year. I don't want to get an F on my report card."

"I'm sorry to hear that," Ms. Allen said. "I understood from Mr. Coronado that you were doing better."

"I'm still struggling," Tamera said. "By next fall I'll be older and wiser and more mature, and then maybe I'll understand it all better."

"And what do you want to switch to?" Ms Allen asked.

"Auto shop."

Ms. Allen paused for a moment. "We don't often get girls who want to take auto shop. I'd have to warn you that you'll probably be given a hard time by the boys in that class."

"I don't care. It would be worth it," Tamera said with a happy sigh. "Could I just try it this afternoon, please?"

"I suppose you could. . . ." Ms. Allen said hesitantly.

"And then I thought I'd switch from art to band," Tamera said hastily.

Ms. Allen looked interested. "Why, Tamera, I didn't even know played an instrument."

"Played an instrument?" Tamera hadn't thought of that. "Oh, right. No, I've never played an instrument, but I've always wanted to. It's been one of my dreams. Along with auto shop."

"Which instrument have you dreamed of playing?"

"Which instrument? Oh, let's see . . ." She went through all the instruments she could think of. They all seemed too difficult. "The triangle," she said at last. "I've always wanted to play the triangle."

Ms. Allen was beginning to look suspicious. "Are you sure you're not putting me on, Tamera? Is this some kind of dare?"

"Oh no, Ms. Allen," Tamera said. "I'm dead serious. I really do want to get into band, only I've never had any music experience, so I thought the triangle might be a good way to start. I could learn that in a hurry, couldn't I?"

Ms. Allen shook her head. "Tamera, I think one schedule change is enough. Besides, playing in a band really does require knowing how to play an instrument."

"Okay," Tamera said. "I'll just start with auto shop then." She danced out of the guidance office.

"Hey, Tamera, are you coming to lunch?" Tia called to her. "I was looking all over for you."

With a disgusted look on her face, Tamera plunged her hand into the grease. "Gross," she muttered. The boys were still grinning. "Maybe I could have someone help me with this first time around?"

"I'd be delighted to help you, my little flower," said a familiar voice. Roger's head emerged from underneath the truck. "Come down here with me. There's room for two on this dolly."

"Gross!" Tamera said, louder this time.

"Good idea," Mr. Oleary said. "Why don't you show this young lady how we work around here, Roger. You stick with Roger, young lady. You let him show you everything he's learned."

"It will be an honor," Roger said, beaming at Tamera. "Here, my little beauty. You can lie down beside me."

Tamera felt as if her world had turned from dream into nightmare in seconds. Instead of standing and watching Barry and handing him wrenches, she was expected to go under a truck with Roger and dig her hands into grease!

It took her so long to clean her hands at the end of shop that she was late for art. As she stood in the bathroom she noticed that her T-shirt had streaks of grease across it. Her nails were a disgusting mess, and she hadn't even gotten anywhere near Barry. It turned out that he was an advanced student and was working with some other guys on their own project, away from the rest of the class.

Tamera was feeling very down as she went home that night. Fate was keeping her away from Barry, but she wasn't ready to give up yet. Now was the time to make use of Tia's brain power. If anyone could come up with a clever scheme, Tia could.

Tamera came into the house and dropped her book bag on the nearest chair.

"Tamera, is that you?" Ray's voice boomed from the kitchen. "Would you come in here, please?"

Tamera had heard that tone of voice often enough to know that it meant trouble. But she couldn't think of anything she had done wrong, unless Charles had been to the house and confessed to doing her homework.

"Hi, Dad," she said, trying to sound innocent. "What's up?"

"I've just had an interesting call from your school counselor," Ray said, his eyes not leaving Tamera's face for a second. "She called to check with me that it was okay for you to drop science and take auto shop." He glared at Tamera. "Well?" he asked. "Do you mind telling me what this is about?"

"Uh—" Tamera opened her mouth, but no words would come out.

"Since when have you shown any interest in auto shop?" Ray demanded.

"I'm going to be driving soon," Tamera said. "I thought it was about time I learned how cars work."

"You mean you thought it was a good time to get out of a hard science class and take something easier," Ray said. "I know you too well, Tamera. You've been trying to find a way to get out of that science class all year, haven't you?"

Tamera was desperately trying to think whether it would be worse to admit that she dropped the class to be with a boy, or to get out of taking science. She decided to say nothing.

"That isn't what I expect of you, Tamera," Ray went on. "You know that I want you to do well in school. If you're failing science, then we'll get you a tutor. Your counselor suggested someone who could work with you on weekends."

"On weekends?" The nightmare was getting worse. "You want me to do science on weekends?"

"I don't care how long it takes or how much energy you have to put into it, but you're not going to fail science, Tamera."

Tamera sighed. "Okay, Dad. I promise I won't fail science. You don't need to get me a tutor. I'll work extra hard, and Tia can help me."

"Tia has enough to do with her own schoolwork right now. I'm sure we can find someone who would be happy to help you."

"Dad!" Tamera sighed. How could she get out of

this latest nightmare without telling him the truth? "Okay, okay," she said breathlessly. "I wasn't failing science. I switched classes so that I could be with Barry Blackwell."

"Barry Blackwell?"

"The rapper guy I told you about."

Ray shook his head. "Tamera, when are you going to learn that there is more to life than boys? If you put as much energy into your studies as you do into finding dates, you'd be a star student like your sister."

"Did it ever occur to you that I put my energy into other things because I know I can never be a star like Tia?" Tamera demanded. "All I hear every day is how wonderful Tia is and how hopeless I am."

Ray got up and put his arm around his daughter. "I'm sorry, honey. Maybe we haven't been considering your feelings enough when we keep praising Tia. But I really believe that you could do as well as your sister if you only tried. You have this energy and all these creative ideas that you put into things like getting dates with boys. Try using them for your classes for a change, okay?"

He smiled at her and ruffled her hair. Tamera smiled back at him. At least she'd talked her way out of having a science tutor spoiling her weekends. But she now had no way of getting close to Barry.

# Chapter 6

๑๑

When Tamera arrived at school the next morning, the first person she saw was Charles, anxiously waiting by her locker. "Oh, Tamera," he said. "There you are. I'm so relieved. I wondered what happened to you."

"What happened to me when?" Tamera asked.

"Yesterday afternoon. I didn't see you in science so I didn't have a chance to get your math homework from you."

"Whoops," Tamera said. She had been so concerned with getting into Barry's classes that she had forgotten that she sat with Charles in science and gave him her math homework to do. Now she had no math homework to hand in and no time to do it.

"I'm really sorry," Charles said.

Tamera looked at him gazing at her with worried eyes and she began to feel bad. "It's not your fault, Charles," she said. "You're kind enough to help me out. It's my own stupid fault for not getting the assignment to you."

"Tell me what it is now, and I'll try to work on it during first period," Charles said. "I can't promise anything, but I'll do what I can."

"You're a very nice person, Charles," Tamera said.

Charles's face lit up. "Thank you," he said. "I'm glad you think so. I think you're a very nice person, too." They started walking down the hall together. "I was dreading coming to a new school in the middle of the year," he went on, "and you were the only person who smiled at me when I sat next to you. And you have such a wonderful smile, Tamera." He gazed at her hopefully, moving closer to her. "I was just wondering . . ."

Tamera looked up as a noisy group of kids came down the hall toward her. Then her heart skipped a beat as she saw that Barry was in the middle of the group. What's more, Barry was actually looking at her as if he half recognized her. And she realized, to her horror, that she was standing close to a nerd! Now Barry would think that Charles was her boyfriend.

"Well, thanks for your help, Charles," she said in

a loud voice. "Gotta run." And she fled into the nearest girls' bathroom.

Immediately she felt bad about running away from Charles. He was such a nice person. He had looked at her so hopefully. It wasn't his fault that he wasn't Barry. It's not fair, Tamera thought. You can't help who you fall in love with.

She wondered if Tia was working on the perfect plan to get Barry to notice her. She hadn't been too enthusiastic the night before, but then she was still angry at Mr. Wilson and still talking about giving up boys forever. Tamera hoped Tia would soon get over this man-hating stage so that she could be some real help with Barry. Time was running out. Tamera now had less than three weeks to make him notice her, make him fall hopelessly in love with her, and ask her to the dance.

She was still trying to come up with her own brilliant plan when she met her friends and went into the cafeteria for lunch.

"Who's coming shopping this weekend to look for dance dresses?" Michelle asked, looking around the table.

"I'm wearing what I've already got," Sarah said. "I've been going with Adam for months now. I don't have to impress him anymore."

"Well, I certainly need a new dress," Denise said. "I'm thinking of asking Harvey."

"You're going to ask a guy?" Chantal squeaked.

"Sure, why not? This is the nineties, you know," Denise said. "And I know Harvey likes me. He's just a little shy. What he needs is a push."

"How about you, Tamera?" Michelle asked. "Are you coming dress shopping with us?"

"Do you know who you're going with?" Chantal asked.

"I think so," Tamera said.

"Who?"

"It's a secret," Tamera said. She looked across the cafeteria. In the far corner she could see Barry sitting with his friends. He looked so relaxed, so confident, so wonderful, Tamera thought.

"When are you going to tell us?" Chantal insisted.

"When she's managed to find someone," Sarah teased.

"You just wait," Tamera said. "You wait until I make my grand entrance at the dance. Then you'll all be green with envy."

As she watched, Barry went up to the counter and came back with a brownie. Then a wonderful idea hit Tamera. They used student helpers in the cafeteria, didn't they? It was a job not many people wanted—who wanted to waste their whole lunch hour getting zits from grease fumes?

But Tamera was desperate enough to try anything if it brought her in contact with Barry. She got up from the table. "Excuse me, you guys. I

have to go do something," she said, and headed
for the kitchen.

"What do you want?" the grouchy woman who
ran the kitchen asked as Tamera poked her head
in through the kitchen door.

"I was wondering if you needed any student cafeteria helpers right now?" Tamera asked sweetly.

"We always need 'em," the woman growled.
"They're always quitting on me. If I give you the
job, how do I know you won't quit on me, too?"

Tamera gave what she hoped was a sincere smile.
"I'm very reliable," she said. "And I could use the
extra money."

"Huh. You won't get rich on what we pay,
honey," the woman said. "But I'll give you a try.
Show up tomorrow. Twelve-fifteen sharp."

"Yes, ma'am," Tamera said. She danced down
the hallway. At last she had a chance of meeting
Barry!

"Where are you going, Tamera?" Michelle yelled
as Tamera disappeared down the hallway after
fifth period.

"See you guys later. I've got a date with destiny,"
Tamera called. She slipped into the kitchen.

Several other students were already putting on
uniforms. The cafeteria manager spotted Tamera
as she stood in the doorway. "Come on in and get
started," she said. "That's your apron."

Tamera looked in disgust at the shapeless grayish white object. Hardly what Barry would be attracted to, she thought. She put it on over her clothes.

"And don't forget this," the cafeteria manager called.

"What is it?" Tamera asked as the woman held out a brownish object.

"Your hair net and cap," the woman said. "All your hair goes in the hair net. The cap goes over it. Make sure no hair is showing."

"Excuse me?" Tamera wailed. "Do I have to?"

"If you want to work here, you do. And the rubber gloves."

Tamera glanced at her reflection in the polished hood of the grill. How could she dazzle Barry when she was wearing a big white apron and a hair net?

At least I've still got my smile and my personality, she told herself. She pulled the cap as far back as she dared.

"Walter will show you what to do," the manager said.

A shrimpy boy who looked ridiculous in his hair net led Tamera to the counter. "The price of everything is on the board. Don't fill the bowl too full when they want chili. And we don't do custom orders. What they see is what they get."

"Got it," Tamera said.

She glanced down the line as she started filling orders. No sign of Barry. With her luck he'd probably go on a health food kick and never go near the cafeteria again.

The work was hot and tiring. Sweat trickled down Tamera's face. She wiped it off with a greasy glove. Now her face was sweaty and greasy. She must look totally disgusting!

She glanced up to see Michelle, Sarah, and the rest of their friends standing in line.

"Tamera, what are you doing?" Michelle demanded loudly.

"Tamera—that hair net is not you at all," Chantal said, wrinkling her nose.

"Are you out of your mind?" Sarah asked. "Only losers work in the cafeteria."

Tamera tried to give them a mysterious smile. "It's all part of my secret plan," she said. "I hope to be back with you by the end of the week—if I last that long," she added.

The line went on and on. Tamera's feet ached from running between the grill and the counter. Her arm ached from dishing out bowls of chili. What's more, she was starving. And Barry still hadn't shown up.

Finally, when lunch break was almost over, she saw him. Her heart started racing as he got closer to the front of the line. He was wearing a white turtleneck, which highlighted his bronze skin and dark eyes. Tamera had forgotten how gorgeous he was close up.

"Hi," he said. "I'd like a bowl of chili."

"One bowl of chili coming up," Tamera tried to say in her perkiest voice. Instead it came out, "One . . . bowl . . . chili . . ."

"That's right. A bowl of chili. That's not too hard for you, is it?" Barry asked, glancing back at Whitney, who was standing in line behind him.

"Oh no, no problem at all," Tamera stammered. She picked up a plastic bowl and hoped that she glided over to the chili pot. She looked in and couldn't believe what she was seeing. The huge chili pot was empty.

"We need more chili," she called into the kitchen.

"Sorry. We're all out," the manager called back.

Oh no, Tamera thought. How could she disappoint Barry during their first real meeting? She turned back and gave him her brightest smile. "We're almost out of chili, but I think I can just manage to find one bowl for you," she said.

"Great!" Barry gave her a dazzling smile.

She ran the ladle around the bottom of the pan, but it was too large to get into the corners where a small amount of chili remained. Tamera was feeling desperate now. She could feel Barry's eyes on her. It took all her strength to lift the pot, but she managed to turn it upside down. She shook it. Nothing moved. She banged on the bottom, hoping to dislodge that stubborn chili. Nothing happened.

"Don't worry. I'll get some for you," she told Barry with a bright smile.

She thumped even harder. Suddenly there was a squelching noise and splat. The chili landed on the counter, sending red-brown goop flying in all directions.

"Oh no," Tamera wailed.

"Oh no!" Barry echoed at the same moment. "Look what you've done, you idiot!"

Tamera winced. There were red chili spatters all over Barry's white turtleneck. He looked like the victim of a nasty accident.

Whitney stepped forward. "You stupid creep— his turtleneck is ruined!" she yelled. "We were supposed to be going out after school today! How can he go anywhere now?"

It seemed as if a silence had fallen over the whole cafeteria. Everyone had stopped eating and was watching the action at the counter.

"I-I'm really sorry," Tamera stammered. "I was just trying to be helpful. You said you wanted chili. I was trying to give it to you."

"You sure gave it to him all right," one of Barry's friends commented.

"It's not funny," Whitney snapped. "I gave him that shirt as a present. Make that clumsy fool buy you a new one, Barry!"

"It's okay," Barry said, looking embarrassed at the fuss Whitney was making. "I'm sure she didn't mean to. You know these cafeteria helpers." He lowered his voice. "Aren't they usually—you know—special ed students?"

"I don't care who she is. I want her fired right now," Whitney screamed.

"What's happening here?" The cafeteria manager appeared at Tamera's shoulder.

"I had a little accident with the chili," Tamera said, wishing the floor would open up and swallow her. "I was only trying to be helpful. I said I'm sorry."

"It's her first day," the manager said.

"She's totally clueless. Get her out of here before there's real trouble," Whitney insisted.

Suddenly Tia pushed her way through the crowd. "Tamera, what are you doing?" she asked.

Tamera shrugged. "Working in the cafeteria, but I don't seem to be too good at it."

"I'll say," Tia said. "Hold on, I'll come in and help you get that mess cleaned up."

"And then fire her," Whitney said.

"You can't fire her," Tia said angrily. "Because she's quitting."

Tia came in through the swinging door and grabbed Tamera. "Come on, take that stupid hair net off and let's get out of here," she said. She helped Tamera out of the apron and hair net and dragged her out of the kitchen.

"I think you've finally flipped," Tia said once they were safely outside. "What were you doing working in the cafeteria? You don't need money that badly, and if you do, I'll lend you some."

"It wasn't about money," Tamera said. "I only did it to make Barry notice me."

"You sure succeeded in doing that," Tia said.

"You're right." Tamera sighed. "Now he thinks I'm the world's biggest idiot. I wish I could die, Tia."

She sank onto the nearest bench and put her head in her hands. Tia sat beside her and put her arm gently around her sister. "It's not as bad as that," she said.

"Oh no? What could be worse?" Tamera demanded. "I got chili all over Barry's white turtleneck."

"I hope that teaches you a lesson, Tamera," Tia said.

"It sure does," Tamera said.

"I'm glad to hear it," Tia said. "You mean you've finally learned that chasing after guys isn't worth it?"

"No, I've learned that if you want to impress a guy, don't wear a hair net," Tamera said.

"Tamera, you're hopeless!" Tia exclaimed.

"It's true, Tia," Tamera said. "If I had looked totally cute, Barry wouldn't have cared if I'd poured the whole pot of chili on him. He only yelled at me because I was a dork in a hair net. Now I've got to start all over again to try to make him like me."

"Don't tell me you haven't given up on this crazy Barry thing?" Tia spluttered. "After what happened today?"

"Of course I haven't given up," Tamera said. "I'm going to get Barry to notice me or I'm going to die trying!"

# Chapter 7

ॐॐ

"Tia, where are you? Get out here right now!" Tamera yelled as she burst in through the front door after school on Friday afternoon.

"What's happening?" Tia asked, coming out of their bedroom.

"I've got it!" Tamera yelled up the stairs.

"Got what?"

"A way to get together with Barry."

"You're crazy." Tia started to head back to the bedroom again.

"No, wait, I'm serious." Tamera bounded up the stairs two at a time. "I heard him telling someone that he was performing with his rap group tonight at Club X."

"So what's your point?"

"It's obvious. I make myself look gorgeous, go to Club X, and meet him. It's small, it's dark, it's intimate . . ."

"It's off limits to you," Tia finished for her. "You know your dad would never let you go to a place like that."

"But this is an emergency," Tamara said. "Think about it, Tia. It's my big chance to meet Barry on neutral ground. If he sees me at school, he thinks of me as the girl who spilled chili on him or who crashed his auto shop class. If he meets me at Club X and I'm looking good, he'll just see someone new and exciting."

"I think you're crazy, Tamera," Tia said. "Club X isn't in the greatest part of town. You want to risk going there alone at night?"

"Not exactly alone," Tamera said. "I was hoping you'd come with me."

"Are you serious? Why would I want to go to a dance club when I've given up boys?" Tia said.

"But you haven't given up your sister, have you? You wouldn't want me to go all the way across town on a bus, by myself, in the dark to a risky kind of club?"

"You're right. I wouldn't. So don't go."

"I have to go, Tia. It's two weeks to the dance. This is my last chance to sweep Barry off his feet."

"Knowing you, that's exactly what you will do." Tia chuckled. "Just don't take a broom with you."

"Very funny," Tamera said. "This is going to

work, Tia. I know it is. Tonight Barry will just see the new improved Tamera, glowing with confidence and personality. He won't even remember that I'm the one from the school cafeteria. I've made up my mind. I'm going to Club X, no matter what. And if you won't come with me, I'll go alone."

She opened her closet and started taking out clothes, holding them up against herself, then dropping them onto her bed.

"The yellow top with the black skirt? Nah, too much like a bumblebee. The white lacy top? Nah, too old-fashioned." Then her face lit up. "Hey, how about this, Tia? The silver spandex bodysuit . . . with the silver lamé tights and the black leather miniskirt! Yes!"

Tia swallowed nervously as she took in the tiny leather miniskirt, the skimpy sleeveless bodysuit, and the tights. "Tamera, you're going to ride a public bus, dressed like that?"

"So I'll put on a long sweater over it until I get there." She held up a pair of black, platform-soled boots. "Do you think I'll be able to get on and off buses wearing these?"

"Tamera, you can't walk across the room wearing those. You've tried."

"So maybe my ankles have grown stronger since I wore them last time," Tamera said. "I have to wear them—they make me look tall and fashionable."

"With a broken ankle," Tia added.

"I'll manage somehow. If Barry finally falls in love with me, then anything is worth it. Even if I have to risk twisting my ankle, alone, in the middle of the big, dark city with no sister beside me for moral support . . ."

"Okay, I'll come with you," Tia snapped. "I'd never forgive myself if anything happened to you."

"You will?" Tamera flung her arms around Tia. "You're the best sister in the world."

"But don't forget that you owe me one," Tia added.

"How could I forget? I'll be in your debt forever."

"And I'm not dressing like that," Tia said. "I'm wearing ordinary jeans and an ordinary top."

"That's fine. I wouldn't want Barry to have to decide between the two of us," Tamera said. "I've got enough competition with Whitney and every other girl in the universe, without you."

"Don't worry. You're welcome to Barry and every other guy on the planet," Tia said. "What time do you want to leave?"

"Around six-thirty, I guess. It will take us forever to get across town at that time, and I know they start performing at Club X at eight."

"You'd better pray that this is one night when your dad works late," Tia commented, "or you won't be going anywhere."

"You're right. We'd better grab something to eat

before anyone gets home so that we can sneak out later if necessary."

Tamera ran downstairs while Tia was changing into her jeans. She burst into the kitchen and stopped short. Her father was standing at the kitchen counter, fixing himself a sandwich.

"Oh, hi, Dad," she stammered. "I didn't hear you come home."

"Hi, honey. Where's the fire?" Ray asked, smiling at his daughter.

"Fire? What fire?"

"Just an expression, Tamera. I meant that you came flying in here as if you were in a big hurry."

"I am," Tamera said. "I'm starving."

"You kids." Ray sighed. "You can eat and eat, and you never put on any weight."

"So what are you doing home so early?" Tamera asked cautiously. "Are you done for the week?"

"Done? Unfortunately not." Ray shook his head. "I'm short a driver, and I have to go back to work tonight."

"You've got to work tonight? You'll be out all evening? That's great!"

Ray looked puzzled. "Great that I've got to work?"

"Oh no, I didn't mean great that you've got to work. I meant, uh, not great at all. That's bad. That's what I was trying to say."

Ray gave her a sidelong glance. "Do you have plans for this evening?"

"Plans? Me? Just hanging out with Tia."

"That's nice," Ray said. "I'm glad that you and your sister enjoy spending time together."

"Me, too," Tamera said. "This evening wouldn't be the same without her."

She finished fixing a sandwich and ran back upstairs. "Phew, that was lucky," she said, closing the door behind her. "My dad has to work tonight. He'll be out all evening. *Yes!* Now I know it's my night."

Tia shook her head. "I'd better make myself a big sandwich. I have a feeling I'm going to need all the energy I can get," she said.

"I'm beginning to think this was a very bad idea, Tamera," Tia whispered as she grabbed her sister's arm. The nearest bus stop had been several blocks away from Club X, and they had been holding on to each other as they walked through deserted city streets.

"I'm just glad I didn't try to do this in my boots," Tamera whispered back.

There was nobody else around, but it seemed safer to whisper, somehow.

"Even when we lived in the city, I never went into this neighborhood," Tia went on. "Even people from this neighborhood never hung around this neighborhood."

"The club's okay. In fact it's famous. Big names perform there," Tamera said. "Only one more block and then we're there."

"Famous last words," Tia muttered as a car screeched past them and a guy yelled something out of the window.

At last they could see the Club X sign flashing ahead of them. Cars were pulling up outside. Normal-looking people were getting out, laughing as they went inside.

"See, it's just fine," Tamera said, letting out a sigh of relief. "Hold on a second. I need to put my boots on."

She balanced herself against Tia as she wriggled into the platform-soled boots. "And take my sweater off," she added, pulling it over her head. "There—how do I look?"

"Different," Tia answered carefully. "Not like you at all."

"Okay, let's do it," Tamera said. "Watch out, Barry, here I come!"

She tottered on the uneven sidewalk and would have fallen over if Tia hadn't grabbed her. "Whoops!" She giggled. "I wish I could get the hang of these things."

"You'd better hold on to me, or you'll never make it in one piece," Tia commented. "Okay, ready? Left, right. Left, right."

They approached the entrance. Two big door-men were standing there, checking people as they went in.

"Let's see your ID," Tamera heard one of them growl.

"I forgot to bring my ID, but I'm really eighteen," they heard a girl in line ahead of them say. "Ask any of these guys. They're in my classes at school."

"No ID, no entrance," the doorman said. "Read what it says."

Tamera pulled Tia aside. "What do we do?" she wailed.

"Not get in," Tia said. "We're not eighteen."

"Why didn't we think to borrow fake IDs?" Tamera groaned.

"Because we don't know anybody who has a fake ID," Tia suggested. "You might have found out you had to be eighteen to get in before we started this nightmare, Tamera."

"I'm not going home now," Tamera said. "Do you think they'd let us in if I said we were with the band?"

"No."

"How about you pretend to have an accident and keep the doormen busy while I slip inside?"

"Are you crazy? I'm not doing anything like that. Face it, Tamera, you're not going to get in."

"I am, too," Tamera said. "Love and Tamera Campbell do not know the meaning of the word *impossible!*" She looked up and down the darkened street. "There has to be a stage entrance where the bands bring in their equipment. Let's check around the back."

"I'm not walking down that alley," Tia said, trying to grab Tamera as she started down a narrow passageway beside the club.

But Tamera was already clomping down the alley in her high boots, holding on to the building to steady herself. Tia gave a big sigh as she followed.

"Now are you satisfied?" Tia asked as they reached the back of the building and found the only door locked. "Can we please go home?"

"Wait," Tamera said, looking hopefully. "Look, there's a window open. If I could get my hand in and push it up more, then maybe I could—"

"Tamera, you're not going to . . . Tamera, don't even think of . . . Tamera, come back here right now!" Tia said, but Tamera kept struggling with the window until it was open wide enough to get her head and arms in and then to haul herself inside.

"Don't think I'm getting in that way. It's called breaking and entering," Tia called after her sister. "A prison record wouldn't look too great on my college applications and—" She broke off. "Tamera? Are you okay? Tamera, answer me!"

She rushed up to the window and peeked into the darkness of the room beyond. There was no sign of Tamera.

# Chapter 8
∞

*T*amera, where are you?" Tia called into the darkness. "If you're playing games with me, you're in big trouble. Answer me right now."

There was silence.

"Ohmygosh, what am I going to do?" Tia wailed. Why wasn't Tamera answering her? All kinds of horrible ideas were going around inside Tia's head. What if it wasn't just an ordinary room in there? What if it was a hangout for a gang or a shaft leading down to who knew what? She looked hesitantly at the open window. Should she go in after Tamera? But what could she do if Tamera really was in trouble? It would make more sense to go for help, she decided. "I'll have to go back to the front door and tell them. I just hope they'll believe me."

She started back toward the alleyway. She was just turning the corner when the big steel door opened behind her. Tia almost jumped out of her skin. She was too scared to run.

"Are you going to stay out there all evening?" Tamera's voice asked.

Tia spun around. "What happened to you? You didn't answer me. I was scared out of my mind!"

"I went to find the door," Tamera said. "That was only a storage closet. Come on in. We're at the back of the club. I can hear the music and everything. All we have to do is find our way around to the front without anyone seeing us."

"Is that all?" Tia muttered. "No problem in that."

She slipped in through the door Tamera held open for her. They were in a dimly-lit passageway with closed doors on either side. From around a corner they could hear the heavy beat of music.

"I guess it has to be down here," Tamera said. "Come on. If anyone stops us, we say we're with the band."

Tia opened her mouth to say something, then closed it again. It looked as if there was no way she was going to talk sense into Tamera right now. They reached the corner. Another passageway led toward a glow of light. The music was louder now.

They crept forward. They had gone only a few steps when they heard voices in the passage behind them. A blast of cold air told Tia that door had been opened again. Someone had come in. They were trapped.

"Maybe they won't come this way," Tamera said as the voices got nearer.

"Thanks for driving us, man," a deep voice was saying. "We should be through here by ten. You can sit out front until we're done if you like. We've got a table."

"Thanks, but I'd better go move the limo," another voice replied. "Do you need help carrying in this equipment?"

Tamera looked at Tia in horror. "My dad!" she whispered. "This was the job he had tonight! What am I going to do, Tia? If he finds me here, he's going to kill me. I'll be grounded for the rest of my life!"

Shadows appeared on the wall as the speakers headed for Tia and Tamera. Tamera grabbed Tia's arm and dragged her in the direction of the lights and music. At the last second Tia managed to stop her. The passageway led directly onto the stage! They could see the drummer's back as he beat out the rhythm.

"Quick, in here," Tia whispered. She opened the nearest door and dragged Tamera inside. She only just managed to shut it as they heard Ray's voice in the passage behind them.

"That was close," Tamera gasped.

"I'll say," Tia agreed. "Boy, you sure like to live dangerously, don't you? This is the last time I go along with one of your crazy schemes, Tamera."

"At least we're safe in here," Tamera said, looking around the room. It was a kind of primitive dressing room, with a mirror and clothes rack and a couple of chairs at a rickety table. "We just have to hang out here until my dad goes. You don't suppose he'll come back when he's parked his limo, do you? Nah, he wouldn't do that, would he? He hates this kind of music."

"It's pretty chilly out there, Tamera," Tia pointed out.

"Don't say that. If he's here, there's no way I can show my face all evening, and Barry's going to be performing soon."

She opened the door a fraction of an inch. The hallway was empty. The music had stopped.

"If you just joined us, welcome to local talent night," an announcer was booming. "It's all happening here tonight! We're jammin'." Loud cheers interrupted this speech. "And now I want you to meet a little lady who's headed straight for the top. Club X is proud to present Princess Phoenicia!"

There was more loud cheering. Suddenly the door was wrenched out of Tamera's hands. She gasped as a guy in a dark turtleneck grabbed her. "Get out there. You're supposed to be on," he yelled.

Tamera was too shocked to speak as he dragged her out of the room. "Wait, you've made a mistake, I'm not—" she managed to say as she was rushed down the hall. "Get out there," the guy said, and gave her a shove. Tamera staggered out into the bright spotlight. She stood there in horror as she realized she was onstage with hundreds of half-visible faces staring at her.

Any second she expected her father to leap up from the audience and demand to know what she was doing there.

"I-I'm sorry," she stammered, turning to the surprised-looking band. "This is a mistake. I'm not . . ." She stopped as another girl came onto the stage. This one was clearly a performer. She was wearing a skin-tight red sequined dress and fake eyelashes a mile long. She stopped when she saw Tamera.

"What do you think you're doing?" she demanded.

"Getting out of here," Tamera said. "I came out here by mistake. Don't worry. I'm leaving." She tried to back away, but she found that she wasn't very good at backing up in her new boots. Tamera backed but the boots stayed where they were. One second she was standing up, the next she had fallen over like a tree. As she fell she hit the cymbals. They toppled over too with a loud crash. Tamera heard a roar of laughter from the audience.

As she staggered to her feet, she heard more laughter coming from the wings. She looked up and there was Barry, standing with his group and Whitney.

"I know you from somewhere, don't I?" Barry asked as Tamera rushed offstage.

"Me? No. Never saw you before in my life," Tamera said, wishing she could get out of there as quickly as possible.

"Hey, it's that klutzy girl from school who spilled chili on you, Barry," one of his friends said.

"It is!" Whitney agreed. "Does she go around making a fool of herself everywhere, do you think?"

Tamera pushed past them.

"Hey, baby, if you want to be a clown, try the circus," Barry called after her as his friends kept on laughing.

"That's where she belongs—the freak show," she heard Whitney's high voice. "What a loser!"

Tamera flung herself into the room where Tia was still waiting. "You were right," she said. "Big mistake. I should never have come here."

Tia put her arm around Tamera. "Come on," she said. "Let's go home."

\*　　\*　　\*

"I'm doomed, Tia," Tamera muttered as they sat on the bus together. "Every time I'm close to him, something terrible happens. Why can't he ever see me like a normal person?"

"I think you were lucky that nothing worse happened tonight," Tia said. "We didn't get mugged, we didn't get arrested for sneaking into that club, and your dad didn't see us. You should be happy."

"How can I be happy when I did the famous collapsing person routine in front of the guy I adore? What can I ever do to make him think of me differently?"

"Give up on him, Tamera. You're wasting your time," Tia said. "He's got a girlfriend, and he's not going to ask you to the dance, even if you learn to fly and drop in beside him by parachute."

"Now, that's a thought," Tamera said. "I wonder who gives parachute lessons?"

# Chapter 9

❧

"Listen up, guys. I've got an important piece of news for you," Mr. Wilson said as he swept into Tia's math class the next Monday morning. "I've just had a talk with the principal and . . ."

Tia's heart leaped. Maybe Principal Vernon had finally taken some action and set Mr. Wilson straight about his antigirl attitude.

". . . and it seems we've had a challenge from St. Joseph's High School."

"They want us all to become priests?" a voice from the back joked.

"An interschool math competition," Mr. Wilson said. "They heard about our mathletes, and they thought it was a great idea. Principal Vernon wants me to pick a team of three guys from this class to compete against the boys of St. Joe's." He looked around the room. "So start thinking who you want to represent this school. Okay, on to the graphs we were having trouble with last week."

Tia glanced across at Joanie Chen as Mr. Wilson started writing on the board. Joanie rolled her eyes and shrugged.

The moment the bell rang Tia went over to Joanie. "Did I hear right? Did he say he wanted us to pick three 'guys' from this class?"

"It sounded like that to me," Joanie said.

"Me, too," Wendy Rosenthal agreed.

Tia noticed that all seven girls in the class had come over to join them.

"I think we should straighten this out right now," Tia said.

"Good luck," Wendy said. "I've tried talking to him, and it's like hitting my head against a brick wall."

"Maybe if we all went up to him together," Joanie suggested.

"Good idea." Tia headed straight for Mr. Wilson's desk. He looked up with a pleasant smile. "Yes, ladies? Got something you don't understand?"

"That's right," Tia said.

Mr. Wilson's smile broadened. "And too shy to ask about it in front of the boys, right? That's okay.

Don't feel bad. It's a known fact that girls have a harder time with advanced math. It has to do with right and left brain thinking."

"No, it has to do with right and wrong brain thinking," Tia said. Joanie and Wendy glanced at her and grinned. "Mr. Wilson, did we understand correctly that you said you wanted us to pick three guys to represent this class? Or did you really mean three students to represent this class?"

"Come on, girls, give me a break here," Mr. Wilson said, laughing uneasily. "It's nothing personal, I assure you. If we're going against a boys' academy it makes more sense to have boys representing us, doesn't it?"

"Not at all. It makes more sense to have the three best students representing us," Wendy said sweetly. "And I'd say that Tia was one of the three best students."

"It's also a question of handling pressure," Mr. Wilson said. "Everyone knows that boys are calmer in a crisis situation. That's why guys are in the army. They don't lose their heads and have hysterics."

"I don't believe this," Joanie muttered. "Mr. Wilson, you are the most sexist person I've ever met."

"It's just the way I am, young lady. I can't help what I think. You take me or leave me. There are other math teachers in this school."

"Maybe there will be one less math teacher by the time we've finished," Tia said. She turned to the other girls. "Come on, let's get out of here. It's time we showed that we're not taking this kind of stuff any longer."

She stalked out of the classroom. The other girls followed her.

"What are you going to do, Tia?" Joanie asked.

"Let the world know what we have to put up with here."

"How are you going to do that?" Renee Jones asked nervously.

"What do people do when they've got a grievance?" Tia asked.

"Walk up and down with signs?" Joanie suggested.

"Then let's start with that," Tia said. "If we walk up and down outside the front entrance with signs, at least the rest of the school will know what's going on. With any luck a local radio or TV station will get to hear about it. If we made the local news, they'd have to fire Wilson."

"Wow! You want to get Mr. Wilson fired?" Renee asked.

"If he's not going to change," Joanie said, "I agree with Tia. We shouldn't have to put up with this. Let's do it."

"Yeah, let's start right now," Wendy said. "I

know the art teacher pretty well. Maybe she'd give us some boards and markers."

Tia ran down the hall beside Wendy, feeling excited and scared at the same time. She had never done anything like this before, but then she had never felt so strongly about anything in her whole life.

Wendy came out of the art room with poster boards and big markers. "I told Ms. Hammersly that I'd replace them tomorrow," she said. "I didn't want to get her in trouble."

"What are we going to put on them?" Renee asked.

"How about 'Mr. Wilson's unfair to girls'?" Wendy suggested.

"That's good," Tia said. "How about 'Girls have equal rights to advanced classes'?"

"I know what I'd like to put," Joanie said with a wicked smile, "but I don't want to get in extra trouble for using bad language!"

They worked quickly, printing slogans on their boards.

"Now let's go walk up and down outside the front entrance," Tia said. "That should really make the principal sit up and take notice."

"Or expel us," Renee added.

"He can't expel us for expressing our opinions. That's why we live in the United States of

America," Joanie said. "Come on, let's get out there before lunch hour is over."

Tamera was sitting alone, eating her lunch on a bench outside. She had stayed far away from the cafeteria. In fact she didn't think she'd ever go near the cafeteria again.

Why did everything have to go so stupidly wrong? she asked herself. She was beginning to face the fact that she'd never have a chance with Barry. There was no way he'd ever ask a loser who spilled chili and fell over on the stage to a dance with him, even if he did break up with Whitney.

If only there was some way to change her image, to make Barry see her in a new light. But Tamera had no idea what that might be. Tia hadn't been helpful all weekend. She had told Tamera she was wasting her time.

Tamera wondered where Tia had gone. She hadn't shown up at her locker after morning classes. Come to think of it, the school yard was kind of empty, even though it was a fine day. Where was everybody?

Tamera finished her sandwich and got up. She started to go into the building when she heard shouting coming from the front of the building. She hurried around the building, then stopped in her tracks. A group of girls was marching around at the foot of the front steps. They were chanting, "Mr. Wilson has to go. Hee hee hee. Ho ho ho!"

It took Tamera a moment to realize that one of them was Tia!

A crowd had gathered to watch the girls. Some of them called out in encouragement. Others weren't so polite.

"What's going on here?" A voice behind Tamera made her freeze. It was Barry, and he was standing right behind her. "It's not the cheerleaders practicing, is it?"

"Are you serious?" Definitely Whitney's voice. Tamera would recognize it anywhere. "Take a look at them, Barry. Total losers."

"They're protesting about some math teacher," a boy said to Barry. "He's unfair to girls."

"Protesting about a math teacher? Are they nuts?" Barry chuckled.

"Hey, Barry. Look!" Whitney shrieked. "It's the girl who spilled the chili over you and who fell down at the club."

Tamera closed her eyes and wondered if she should just slink away or stay where she was and pretend that she hadn't heard them.

"I wonder what stupid thing she'll do next?" Whitney went on.

"I didn't think she was smart enough to be in Mr. Wilson's math class," Barry said.

Suddenly the truth hit Tamera—they thought Tia was her!

"You know how smart people can be clueless socially," Whitney said.

Barry chuckled. "You'd have to be pretty clueless to walk around with a sign about math classes."

Tamera wanted to say something. It wouldn't help her much to turn around and tell Barry that she wasn't the smart twin, just the clueless one.

"Hey, Barry." She heard a deep voice behind her. "Did you find a new rap for that talent contest yet?"

"Nah. I've been working on it, but I haven't come up with anything yet. It's hard, man. I think I've used up all my good ideas. I can only write when I'm in the mood."

"So you won't enter the contest then?"

"Not unless I can come up with something really good," Barry said.

Their voices drifted away until they were lost in the crowd. Tamera stood there with a big smile spreading across her face. Finally she might have a way to make Barry think differently about her!

Tamera was waiting for Tia at her locker after school that afternoon.

"Hi," she said. "Did you see our protest march at lunchtime?"

"I saw it," Tamera said. "So did everyone else."

"Great," Tia said. "Nothing has happened yet, but Mr. Wilson must have heard about it. I hope he's doing some serious thinking right now. We'll teach him to think that girls don't matter. We're going to keep on doing it until we get some action."

"Like what?"

"Hopefully the principal will tell Mr. Wilson to shape up or get fired. I'm sure the last thing the principal wants is bad publicity for his school— and you know a TV news show would just love a story like this."

"So you're going to keep on doing it?" Tamera asked, wincing.

"Sure. We have to, for the sake of girls everywhere."

"Not this girl," Tamera said.

"Look, Tamera, I know you're not really into math, but—" Tia began, but Tamera cut her off.

"Do you know who saw your protest today? Barry did. And do you know what he thought?"

"Tamera, I don't really care what Barry thought."

"You should," Tamera said. "He thought that you were me."

"So?" Tia paused at the door, hoisting her backpack onto her shoulder.

"So?" Tamera shrieked. "Tia, he thinks I'm a brainy geek now!"

"I don't see that that's so bad," Tia said. "Isn't it one step up from a hopeless klutz?"

"It's not funny, Tia," Tamera wailed. "It's one more strike against me."

"You know what I think, Tamera," Tia said, walking ahead of her to the bus stop. "I think you're wasting your time over a guy who isn't worth it."

"He is too worth it."

"No guy is worth it," Tia said. "The other girls from my math class totally agree with me. Guys are a pain we can do without. The other girls aren't going to the dance either."

"Only because they're geeks and nobody has asked them," Tamera said.

"Tamera, you shouldn't talk like that," Tia said as they reached the line at the bus stop. "They are very nice girls."

"But geeky," Tamera muttered. "Barry thought they were geeky." She sighed loudly.

Tia looked at her with sympathy. "I'm sorry," she said, "but there's nothing I can do, Tamera."

Tamera's face brightened. "As it happens, there *is* something you can do."

Tia back away. "Oh no. No more dance clubs and climbing through windows. I've had enough excitement for one year."

"Nothing like that," Tamera said. "I just want you to write me something."

"Your homework?"

Tamera glanced around to see if anyone was listening. She leaned close to Tia. "A rap for Barry."

"You want me to write a . . ." She tried to say "rap for Barry," but Tamera clamped her hand over Tia's mouth.

"Shh. I don't want anyone to hear," she said. "Listen to this, Tia. I know that Barry is looking for a new rap so that he can enter a talent contest next week. He's been trying to come up with something and he can't. We all know that you're a terrific writer with a great brain, so I just thought that maybe . . ." She looked pleadingly at Tia. "That maybe you could write me a little rap . . . just a tiny one. And then I could give it to Barry and he'd win the contest and think I was okay after all."

"Tamera, do you know how much homework I have?" Tia demanded.

Tamera swallowed hard. "Okay, how about this? I'll help you with your protest, if you write me a rap."

"How can you help me?" Tia asked.

"I know people. I could get more girls involved. We could get all the girls in the school to join in."

Tia's face lit up. "You really think so?"

"I don't see why not," Tamera said. "Most of us don't have Mr. Wilson, but we know what you're going through. I know I wouldn't put up

with a teacher who didn't want me in his class."
She paused. "Come to think of it, most teachers
don't want me in their class," she said.

Tia smiled. "That's really sweet of you, Tamera,"
she said. "It would be great if we could get enough
girls out there, protesting, so that we made a real
statement." She stared out across the street. "Okay,
I'll try to write you a rap," she said. "Even though
I think you're still wasting your time. From what
I've seen of Barry, he'll take the rap, say thanks a
lot, and still ignore you."

"But it will be one stage better than laughing at
me, right?" Tamera said. "And it might just work.
Bigger miracles have happened before."

"Yeah, and there's a Santa Claus," Tia muttered
to herself.

# Chapter 10

ॐ

*H*ow's this?" Tia asked after dinner. She came up behind Tamera, who was on the sofa watching TV, and dropped a sheet of paper into Tamera's hands.

Here's the story of a guy who was looking his best
Because he was stepping out to take his driving test . . .

Tamera started reading and a big smile spread across her face.

"Tia, you did it—you wrote me a rap, and it's awesome!" Tamera jumped up and threw her arms around Tia. "This is it—my ticket to Barry and to happiness."

"Don't get your hopes too high," Tia said. "He might not like it."

"Not like it?" Tamera demanded. "Tia, it's great. He'll love it. He'll win the talent contest and decide he can't live without me."

Tia didn't say anything.

"I can't wait to see his face when I give it to him at school tomorrow," Tamera went on. "What are you doing after school? Do you want to come to the mall with me?"

"What for?"

"I need to pick out a dress for the dance," Tamera said. "I have to look just perfect, you know."

Tia put her hand on her sister's arm. "Cool it, Tamera. Even if he likes the rap, it doesn't mean that he's instantly going to ditch Whitney and ask you to the dance instead. Besides, I thought you said you had no money."

Tamera leaned closer to her sister. "There's a little thing called a savings account."

"But that's your college money. Your dad would have a fit if you touched that."

"If I go to the dance with Barry, I don't care what my dad says," Tamera said. "It is my money, after all. And I'm spending it on a good cause."

"I'd hold off on buying the dress if I were you," Tia said. "I'd wait until he asks you to the dance."

"If you believe, it will happen," Tamera said dramatically. "And it's going to happen, thanks to you, my wonderful sister."

Tia went back upstairs. She decided it probably wasn't the right moment to remind Tamera that she had promised to join in the protest at school.

After lunch the next day Tamera sprinted over to the auto shop. The auto shop was one place that Whitney definitely wouldn't be with him. She couldn't imagine Whitney ever getting dirt under her fingernails.

Why should I worry about Whitney? she told herself. She will soon be history.

Tamera waited in the doorway until she saw Barry coming. He was alone for once. Maybe her luck had finally turned!

"Hi, Barry!"

Barry jumped as Tamera stepped out of the shadows.

"Oh, it's you. What do you want?" he asked, looking around nervously.

"I just wanted to give you something," Tamera said, holding out an envelope.

"It hasn't got chili in it, has it?" Barry said with an uneasy laugh.

"Not even close," Tamera said. "I heard you saying that you needed a new rap for a talent show, and it just happens that my sister and I are great at raps. I thought maybe you could use this."

Barry was still holding the envelope away from him as if it might be dangerous. "Uh . . . thanks . . ." he said.

"Tamera," she finished for him. "My name's Tamera. My twin sister, who you have probably seen walking around with a sign outside the front entrance, is called Tia. She looks like me, but we're very different, in every way."

"Oh, okay," Barry said. He gave her a real smile this time. "Thanks for thinking of me, Tamera."

"No problem," Tamera said.

"I'll read it when I get time." He looked up as more guys headed to the auto shop and slipped the envelope into his pocket.

"Sure. Let me know what you think." Tamera gave him a hopeful smile and slipped away as the auto shop teacher walked across the school yard. This was a good start. Barry had taken the envelope. He promised to read the rap. He hadn't thrown it into the nearest trash can.

Tamera spent the rest of the afternoon in suspense. She pictured Barry reading the rap and loving it, then rushing to find her after school was over. "This is the best thing I've ever seen in my life," he'd say. "Why don't I give you a ride home and we can talk about it over a soda?"

But then doubts crept in, and she imagined

Barry reading it and not liking it. "Can you believe what that crazy girl did now?" he'd say. "Look what dumb stuff she wrote for me."

Then Whitney would read it and laugh, too.

Sixth and seventh period went by. Tamera passed the music room where Barry had band, but she couldn't catch a glimpse of him. She hung around the halls after school, but he didn't show up.

It was a great idea while it lasted, she told herself. *I thought the rap was good, but maybe it was too juvenile for someone mature like Barry.*

She decided not to go to the mall that night. She didn't feel in the mood to buy a dress for the dance.

"So what did Barry think of the rap?" Tia asked Tamera when they met at the bus stop.

"I don't know," Tamera said. "I haven't seen him since I gave it to him. I guess he can't have loved it or he would have told me by now. But thanks for trying, Tia. I thought it was really great."

"Don't forget you promised to join my protest tomorrow," Tia said. "And bring all your friends."

"Sure. I'll be there," Tamera said flatly. If Barry didn't like the rap, nothing mattered anymore, even looking like a geek walking around with a sign.

The next morning passed, and Tamera didn't see Barry. At lunchtime she persuaded Sarah, Michelle, and Denise to join in Tia's protest.

"I wouldn't want anyone telling me that he didn't want to teach girls," Sarah said.

"We should get all the girls in the school to join in. That would really make a statement," Michelle added. "If nothing has happened by tomorrow, we'll drag in every girl we know."

Tamera took a sign and started walking. She had been there only a couple of seconds when she saw Barry. Okay, so I look stupid, she thought, but I guess it doesn't matter anymore.

Barry was with a big group of friends, as usual. They were about to pass by when Barry said something to the others and came over to her.

"Tamera?" he asked. "You are Tamera, right?"

Tamera hastily put down the sign. She nodded.

"I read the rap that you wrote," he said. "It was really great. I didn't expect it to be—you know—anything much, so I didn't read it until last night. Then it was like—wow! This is really cool. We're going to do it in the talent show."

"You are?" Tamera felt as if she might burst with happiness any moment.

"It was really great of you to write that for me."

"I just wanted to help," Tamera said modestly.

"That was really nice of you, after I yelled at you about the chili."

"Hey, I'd have been mad too if someone got chili all over my white turtleneck," Tamera said. "I guess I wasn't cut out to be a cafeteria helper."

"No, you're way better as a writer," Barry said. "Do you think you could write more stuff like this? We need new raps all the time now that we're getting gigs at clubs."

"Sure. No problem," Tamera said. "You just tell me what you want, and we'll write it for you."

"Cool," Barry said. "Gotta go. See you around, Tamera."

"*Yessss!*" Tamera yelled as soon as Barry had disappeared.

She ran over to Tia. "Did you see that? He loves the rap. He wants more. He likes me. Pinch me. I'm in heaven, Tia. Do you want to come shopping this afternoon?"

"Did he ask you to the dance?"

"Uh . . . no, not yet. But we only just met. How about you write a rap for me about two people who go to a dance together as friends and wind up falling in love. That might give him the hint."

"Oh please," Tia said with a disgusted look. "Pick up your sign and start marching, okay?"

Tamera picked up her sign, but she was already planning like crazy in her head. She saw the kind of dress she wanted—short and slinky, silver lamé maybe, and Barry in a white tux beside her with a red rose in his buttonhole.

"Okay, we did it," Tamera announced as she and Tia burst into the house that night. "Major shopping accomplished. Anyone want to see the world's most perfect dress?"

Ray and Lisa were already sitting at the dining table. They looked up as Tamera pulled a sleek silver minidress from its bag. "Ta-da! And shoes to match," she said, holding up silver sandals. "And wait, there's more . . . a silver flower for my hair. Is this cool or is this cool?"

"It looks lovely, Tamera," Lisa said. "Doesn't it, Ray?"

"It looks expensive, Tamera," Ray said. "Who is paying for all this?"

"I . . . uh . . . dipped into my savings a little," Tamera said.

"Tamera, you know that account is for college," Ray said.

"Daddy, you want me to look good at the dance, don't you? Self-esteem is very important when it comes to good grades and getting into college."

"Of course she needs a new dress for the dance, Ray. Don't be such an old fuddy-duddy," Lisa said. "So who is the lucky guy, Tamera?"

"The rapper I told you about," Tamera said.

"He hasn't asked her yet," Tia interrupted.

"No, but he's going to." Tamera glared at Tia to shut up. She hoped Tia wouldn't mention Barry by name. She didn't want Ray to put two and two together.

"Tamera, you bought a dress before anyone asked you to the dance?" Ray asked.

"He's going to," Tamera answered. "He just needs to find the right moment."

"So, Tia, honey, did you get a dress, too?" Lisa asked quickly, sensing that Ray was about to explode.

Tia shook her head. "I'm not going."

"Not going to the dance? Why not? Couldn't find a date, honey?"

"Mom, I'm like you. I've given up guys."

"Given up guys—who said anything about giving up guys?"

Tia looked horrified. "You did, Mom. Last week, remember?"

"That was last week, honey," Lisa said. "I met the cutest guy yesterday at the coffee shop. We have a date for Saturday night."

"Mom, you're hopeless," Tia said angrily.

Lisa came up behind her and put a hand on her shoulder. "Tia, honey. Girls of your age should be having fun. Forget this nonsense about giving up men. It's not right."

"I don't get you, Mom," Tia snapped. "We were both treated badly by guys. You might have forgotten about it, but I haven't."

"Tia, baby," Lisa said softly. "I have been known to lose my cool occasionally when I'm upset and say a few things I don't mean." She glared as Ray made a coughing noise in his throat. "One bad apple doesn't really spoil the whole barrel, you know."

Ray's cough turned to a chuckle.

"And I don't know what you're finding so funny, Mr. Know-it-All," Lisa snapped.

Tia started to walk away. "You can change your mind if you want," she said, "but I'm not going to. I'm definitely not going to the dance."

"In that case," Tamera said hopefully, "can I borrow your blue jacket?"

# Chapter 11

◉◉

*H*ey, Tia, look!" Tamera yelled the next morning as Tia stood at her open locker. "I just bought my dance ticket."

Tia looked confused. "I don't get it, Tamera. If Barry asks you to the dance, won't he buy your ticket? And if he doesn't ask you, you won't want to go, will you?"

"I just want to be prepared, that's all. In case all the tickets are sold when Barry asks me. Now I'm all set—I've got the dress, the shoes, the tights, the flower for my hair, and the ticket."

"Now all you need is a date," Tia said dryly.

"It will happen, I know it will," Tamera said.

"You've only got a couple of days, Tamera," Tia said. "Face it, he's not going to ask you."

"You should see how he smiled at me yesterday, Tia," Tamera said. "He said he's dying for me to write more raps for him. He was so excited to win the contest. He said it was a shame I wasn't there to see him. Now, is that progress or what?"

"Nothing's changed, Tamera. He's still with Whitney. He just likes the raps, not you as a person."

"I don't care what you think," Tamera said. "I still believe it's going to happen."

She clutched her dance ticket close to her as she walked to her first class. She didn't care what Tia thought. Tia was wrong. A little voice inside her head whispered that Tia had been right about one thing—there were only two more days and she still didn't have a date. What if Barry didn't ask her? Tamera thought about the silver dress and how good she would look wearing it. She imagined how Barry's eyes would light up and he would say—

"There you are, love of my life! I've been looking everywhere for you."

Tamera spun around and there was Roger, running after her.

"See what I've got here, my little flower?" he called, waving a piece of paper in his hand. "Two tickets to paradise."

"What are you talking about?" Tamera took a quick step backward.

"Dance tickets. You and me, my strong, manly arms around you," Roger went on, beaming at her.

"Are you out of your mind, Roger? Do you really think I'd go to the dance with you?"

"You don't have a better offer," Roger said. "I know. I've been checking on you. And the dance is only two days away. It's me or nobody, honeybun. And you could do worse."

"I can't think how," Tamera muttered. Then she raised her voice so that passersby could hear. "It's very kind of you, Roger, but I already have a fantastic date for the dance."

"Oh yeah—who?" Roger demanded.

"You'll see when we make our grand entrance," Tamera said with a mysterious smile. She hurried on down the hall and almost collided with Whitney.

"Well, look who it is," Whitney said smoothly. "It's the little rap girl." She blocked Tamera's way. "Don't think it's not totally obvious why you're doing this," she went on. "You want Barry to notice you. But let me tell you right now that you're wasting your time. Barry and I have been an item since way back. He's not interested in other girls—especially not losers who make fools of themselves in public."

"Why are you telling me this, Whitney? Could

it be you're feeling worried?" Tamera hoped that she sounded equally smooth.

"Worried? Me?" Whitney laughed. "Why would I have to worry about you? You don't stand a chance."

"That's not how I see it, Whitney," Tamera went on, trying to stay as cool as Whitney.

"Listen, honey," Whitney said, smiling at Tamera like a cat who has just caught a mouse. "He'll string you along because he's naturally lazy and he'd love someone else to write his raps for him. That's how Barry is—a great user. But don't get your hopes up, will you?"

She swept by Tamera, tossing back her black braids.

Tamera found the social studies room and collapsed into her seat. Now that Whitney had gone, she felt sick and scared inside. For the first time she began to have serious doubts. She had really convinced herself that a miracle was going to happen. Now she began to wonder if she had been making a total fool of herself. The more she thought about it, the more she realized that there was no way Barry was going to ask her to the dance. She'd been living in a fantasy.

Tamera felt her face get hot with embarrassment. She was stuck with the ticket, the dress, and all the other stuff—and no possible date except Roger!

She tried to concentrate while Mr. Berry, the

social studies teacher, droned on, but all she could think of was Whitney and Barry dancing together while she danced with Roger. She glanced up as a shadow fell on her.

"Oh, hi, Charles," she said.

He was looking at her with concern. "Didn't you hear the bell? Everyone's gone."

Tamera looked around the empty room. "They have? Oh, right. Sorry. I've got something on my mind right now, Charles."

"Anything I can help you with?" he asked.

Tamera smiled. "It's not as simple as math homework," she said. "That's either right or wrong. This is way more complicated."

"I see," he said. He followed Tamera out of the classroom.

"But don't get me wrong," Tamera said quickly. "I really appreciate what you've been doing for me, Charles. You're a great guy."

"Tamera, I've been wondering," Charles began hesitantly. "This is probably a stupid question because you're so popular . . . but I wondered if you'd come to the dance with me . . . if you don't already have a date, which I'm sure you do."

Tamera looked up at Charles's hopeful face. He certainly wasn't a Barry, but he wasn't a total loser either. He had a nice smile and soulful brown eyes behind his heavy-framed glasses. In fact he reminded her of a shy but friendly puppy, the way he was looking at her now.

And it's him or Roger, she reminded herself.

She took a deep breath. "Sure, Charles. I'd love to go to the dance with you."

His whole face lit up. "You would? Tamera, that's wonderful. It's awesome. It's totally amazing."

"Don't overdo it," Tamera said hastily. "It's not that amazing. We're friends, aren't we?"

"Yeah, but . . . I thought you were out of my league," Charles said. "You've made me so happy, Tamera. What kind of flowers do you like? I want to get you the best corsage. Would roses be okay, or orchids?"

"I don't know . . . I've never had a corsage before," Tamera stammered. "Surprise me."

"Okay, I will," Charles said. "This is great, Tamera. See you Saturday then."

He hurried off, leaving Tamera staring after him. At least I have a date for the dance now, she thought. And Charles is nice. He's just not Barry.

"Tamera, wait up," Tia yelled after her. She fought her way through the crowded hallway and reached Tamera. "It's finally happened, Tamera," she gasped.

"You got asked to the dance?" Tamera asked.

"No way," Tia said, making a face. "I've told you I'm not going. The principal wants to meet with the girls from Mr. Wilson's class on Monday morning. He says he's come up with a way to solve our problem. That has to mean he's reassigning Mr. Wilson, right?" She grabbed Tamera's shoulders. "I am so happy, Tamera. Finally we're being heard. Our protest paid off. I want to thank you for getting more girls to join us. That really helped.

"Sure, no problem," Tamera said.

"I guess Barry hasn't asked you yet," Tia asked gently.

Tamera shook her head. "You were right all along. He's not going to. I was just fooling myself, wasn't I?"

"Stranger things have happened," Tia said.

"It's okay," Tamera went on. "I just told Charles that I'd go with him."

Tia smiled. "Hey, that's great, Tamera. Charles seems like a really nice guy. You'll have a good time with him."

"He does have one advantage," Tamera said. "He's not Roger."

That night Tamera tried on the silver dress.

"What do you think?" she asked Tia.

"Looks great on you," Tia said, looking up from her homework.

"I was thinking of taking it back," Tamera said. "I mean, now that I'm not going with Barry, it doesn't really matter what I wear, does it? And it did cost a lot of money and my dad is still mad at me."

"But you told me that Charles is buying you a corsage. He's so excited about going with you, Tamera. I think you should look good for him. And you might make Barry sorry that he didn't ask you."

"Yeah," Tamera said. "Okay, I'll keep it. I'm going to be the hottest babe at that dance."

On Friday afternoon Tamera was stuffing her books into her locker when Charles came up to her.

"I just wanted you to know that I've ordered your corsage. It's white roses. I hope that will be okay?"

"It will be perfect, Charles," Tamera said. "I'm wearing silver."

"Great!" Charles beamed at her. "I'd come to your house to pick you up, but I don't drive yet," he said.

"That's okay. My dad will probably want to drive me anyway. He's kind of overprotective."

"Aren't all parents?" Charles asked. "The moment I say I'm going out, my parents want to know what time I'll be home."

"Parents are a pain," Tamera agreed. "So I'll meet you at the dance then. Under the clock in the auditorium? Eight o'clock."

"Sounds great," Charles said. "See you tomorrow. Tamera, you don't know how much I'm looking forward to this."

"Me, too," Tamera said, and found that she really was.

She was hurrying across the parking lot to catch the bus when someone grabbed her. "Hey, Tamera, wait up," a deep voice said.

Tamera spun around, startled. "Oh, Barry . . . it's you," she stammered. She always found it hard to speak when he was around.

"Listen, Tamera—do you want to go to the dance tomorrow?" Barry asked.

For a moment Tamera couldn't believe what she was hearing. She wanted to pinch herself to make sure this wasn't another fantasy.

"You're asking me to the dance?" she blurted out.

Barry shrugged. "I know it's kind of short notice, but . . . uh . . . things have changed with me."

Tamera followed his glance across the parking lot and thought she saw Whitney watching them.

"Sure, Barry. I'd love to go to the dance with you." The words came out in a rush. "I even have my own ticket."

"Great," Barry said. "Okay. See you there. Eight o'clock. Main entrance. Don't be late."

Tamera flew across the school yard. She wasn't conscious of her feet even touching the ground.

I can't believe it. It's really happened, she told herself.

"Tamera, come on, you're going to miss the bus," Tia was yelling. Tamera woke up enough to sprint the last few yards and fling herself on board as the driver was closing the door.

"Tia, you'll never guess what just happened to me," Tamera gasped. "The miracle. It happened."

"What?"

"Barry just asked me to the dance."

"Yeah, right." Tia grinned uneasily.

"I swear it, Tia. He just stopped me outside school and asked me if I'd like to go to the dance with him. Just like that."

"Too bad you had to say no."

"Are you serious? Of course I didn't say no. Why would I do that?"

"Because you already told Charles you'd go with him."

Tamera put her hand up to her mouth. "Ohmygosh. Charles! Being close to Barry totally scrambled my brains. What am I going to do, Tia?"

"Call Barry and tell him you made a mistake and you can't go with him."

"No way," Tamera said. "I've got two dates and one of them is Barry Blackwell. Do you think I'd go with Charles Johnson?"

"But Charles asked you first and you said yes."

"So I'll call *him* and tell him I made a mistake."

"Tamera, Charles is a sweet guy. You can't do that to him," Tia said. "It's not fair."

"And you think its fair to *me* to have to spend the whole evening with Charles when I could be with Barry?" Tamera demanded. "There has to be a way out of this, Tia. You're the one with the brains. You come up with a way out."

"Oh no, Tamera. Not this time," Tia said. "You're always expecting me to get you out of things. You have to figure this out for yourself. You know what I think—I think you made a date with Charles and you should keep it."

Tamera stared out of the bus window as buildings flashed past. In her heart she knew that Tia was right. She could imagine how Charles would feel if she stood him up. She pictured him standing there alone, with the corsage in his hand. But then she thought of Barry, looking cool in a white tux, taking her hand as he led her onto the dance floor. And she knew—there was no way she was going to give up the chance of a date with Barry.

If only I could be in two places at once, Tamera thought. Then suddenly it hit her—there was a way out of this after all.

As soon as they got off the bus, Tamera grabbed Tia. "You told me to figure this out for myself, and I have," she said.

"Great," Tia said.

"Only I'm going to need a little help," Tamera went on.

Tia looked at her suspiciously. "Doing what?"

"Being me."

Tea leaped away. "Oh no. Not that again. Forget it, Tamera."

"But it's the answer, Tia, don't you see?" Tamera pleaded. "It's perfect. You've told everyone you're not coming to the dance. We go dressed alike. You stay with Charles all evening at one end of the auditorium. I'll be with Barry at the other end. It's dark and it's crowded. No one would ever find out."

"I see major problems here," Tia said.

"Like what?" Tamera demanded.

"We go dressed alike, you say? You happen to be wearing a very expensive outfit, Tamera. You know I don't have that kind of money."

"No big deal," Tamera said, waving her arms easily. "We get some silver fabric and we have your mother copy the dress."

"I don't think that my mother—" Tia began, but Tamera stopped her.

"You don't have to look really terrific," she said. "You'll only be dancing with Charles."

"Tamera, the way you talk about Charles is so mean," Tia said, striding ahead of her sister. "I can't believe the way you're going to lie to him."

"He'll never know." Tamera ran to keep up with

her. "He's never spoken to you in his life. He'll just think you are me and he'll have a great time. It's simple, Tia. What could go wrong?"

"That's what we always say when we come up with dumb ideas like this, and something *always* goes wrong. Besides, I hate fooling people."

"Oh, really?" Tamera asked innocently. "Who was the person who begged me to take her place at the science fair while she was out with her boyfriend, and I was stuck explaining DNA to my science teacher? And who was the person who made me take her place at a sleepover at a geeky girl's house, while she went to a very cool party?"

"And every time we got in trouble, Tamera. Don't you think we've learned our lesson by now?"

"I'd say it's about time you paid me back what you owe me, Tia. And you owe me this big time. If you really cared about me, you'd want me to have my one chance with the guy of my dreams. And if you were really the greatest sister in the world . . ."

"Okay, I'll do it," Tia cut in. "I probably should have my head examined, but I'll do it."

Tamera flung her arms around Tia. "Thank you, thank you, thank you," she gasped. "This is going to be the most wonderful night of my life, Tia."

"I hope so, for your sake," Tia muttered.

# Chapter 12

୭୭

"I can't believe I'm doing this," Tia said as she stood in the darkness beside Tamera, watching Ray drive away. From across the school yard came the heavy beat of music. Light streamed out of the open doors at the front of the auditorium. "You say I'm supposed to be the one with brains? I think I should have my head examined."

"You won't regret this, I promise," Tamera whispered back. "You might even have fun."

"Yeah, right," Tia said. "I can't wait for it to be over."

"You know what you've got to do, don't you?" Tamera whispered.

"We've been over it a million times," Tia said.

"I go in, then head for the back of the auditorium, take off my coat, and leave it in the room behind the stage. Then I go find Charles."

"You got it," Tamera said. "Okay, it's eight o'clock. Let me go ahead to meet Barry at the front entrance. Give it a couple of minutes before you come in. And if anyone talks to you, you're Tamera, remember?"

"How could I forget?" Tia said. "Okay, get moving. Meet you at your dad's car at eleven-thirty, if we last that long!"

Tia watched Tamera cross the school yard toward the lighted auditorium until she was lost among the crush of students waiting to go into the dance. When she thought Tamera must be safely inside, she started to follow. Her heart was beating so loudly that she was sure people around her must hear it.

Why am I so scared? Tia asked herself. Charles is a nice guy. It will be so noisy in there that I won't even have to talk to him. We dance together and then we go home. Simple. So why were her knees feeling weak?

Tia flashed her ticket at the guy at the entrance table, then sprinted down the narrow hallway to the bathrooms and the back entrance to the auditorium. So far so good. Nobody she knew had seen her. Inside the bathroom she took off her coat and made sure her hair looked okay.

"Here goes nothing," she said to her image in

the mirror before she went to dump her coat in the back room.

A blast of sound greeted her as she opened the back door and found herself at one end of the auditorium. For a moment she couldn't remember what Charles looked like. She felt the panic rising and looked longingly at the door. This was Tamera's problem. Why should she have to handle it for her?

Then she caught sight of him between the dancing couples. He was standing under the clock, just as he had told Tamera, holding a white corsage in a cellophane box and looking around hopefully.

Tia's heart went out to him. It wasn't fair to play this trick on a nice guy like Charles. She'd go right up to him and tell him the truth.

She started to work her way around the edge of the dance floor, avoiding the flying arms and legs. While she was still quite a way from him, he saw her and his whole face lit up.

"Tamera!" he called. "I'm so glad to see you. Man, do you look great tonight. Here, let me put the corsage on your wrist. My older brother said wrist corsages were safer than ones you had to pin on dresses. I guess he meant that a nervous hand can do a lot of damage with a pin." He gave her a shy smile.

Tia took a deep breath. "Look, Charles, there's something I think you should know . . ." she began. He had the corsage out of its box, and he took her hand to slip it on her wrist.

"I was so worried for a while there that you wouldn't show up," Charles went on. "I know it was probably dumb of me, because you're such a sweet girl, Tamera. Why would you not show up when you said you would?"

Tia opened her mouth again, then shrugged as the elastic of the corsage snapped onto her wrist. "Uh . . . sure," she muttered.

"You want to dance?" Charles asked. "I'm not the world's greatest dancer, but I'm willing to give it a try if you are."

"Sure," Tia said again, wondering if she was sounding like a parrot repeating everything.

They moved out onto the dance floor, and Charles started swaying to the beat of the music. Tia was surprised—he wasn't bad at all; in fact, he moved pretty well. She started dancing with him.

"You're a great dancer, Tamera," Charles yelled over the music.

"You're not so bad yourself," Tia answered.

"Me?" Charles rolled his eyes. "My brothers tell me I look like an octopus!"

"You're doing fine," Tia said, giving him an encouraging smile.

"Maybe it's because I'm dancing with you," Charles said, flashing her a special smile.

When the music stopped Charles took her hand

to lead her through the crowd. "Now I know what explorers must feel like, hacking their way through the jungle," he gasped as they reached the edge of the dance floor.

"And we haven't even found Dr. Livingstone," Tia replied with a grin.

"Yeah. I read this book about the African jungle last year in English. It made me decide I never wanted to go there. It was pretty creepy," Charles began.

"I know. *Heart of Darkness.* I read it, too," Tia said without thinking.

"You did? I didn't know you liked to read."

"The Cliffs Notes," Tia said. "I read the Cliffs Notes on *Heart of Darkness.* For me that's the same as reading the book."

I almost blew it there, Tia thought. "So, uh, do you like to read, Charles?" she asked.

Charles's face lit up again. "I love reading. It's even better than watching videos, because the scenery is better." He stopped and grinned awkwardly. "What I really meant was . . ."

"I know exactly what you mean," Tia said. "You mean that the pictures you get in your head when you're reading are better than anything they can put in a movie."

"Exactly," Charles said. "Of course you probably think that only losers like to read."

"No," Tia said. "I think reading's great . . . if I

don't have to do it, myself," she added. Now she was beginning to feel mad at Tamera. If she didn't have to keep up this stupid act, she could have talked to Charles about books they had read.

"My brothers think I'm weird," Charles said, "just because I actually enjoy things like science and math. I suppose you think that's weird, too, right?"

"No way!" Tia blurted out. "Science is my favorite subject!"

"It is?" Charles looked confused.

Instantly Tia realized what she had said. "Wh-what I meant to say is that . . ." she stammered. *This is so stupid!* She couldn't keep it up any longer. She didn't want to keep it up any longer. Charles was a nice guy, and it wasn't fair to be deceiving him like this.

"The truth is, Charles . . ." she began again.

"You're not Tamera, are you?" he asked before she could say anything more.

Tia shook her head. "I'm her sister, Tia."

"She didn't really want to be with me, so she sent you instead. I get it," Charles said. His face fell.

"She had another date, and she didn't want to let you down, Charles," Tia said gently.

"Same thing. She didn't really want to be with me. I guess I was just fooling myself that she really liked me."

"She does really like you, Charles—as a friend," Tia said. "Who wouldn't like you? You're really nice."

"Yeah, that's me. Good old nice Charles," he said. "It's okay, Tia. You don't have to hang around with me anymore if you don't want to."

Tia touched his arm. "You know what you need, Charles? A little bit of self-esteem. If you really want to know, I'm having a great time with you. I think you're the most interesting guy I've met in a long while."

"Are you serious?" Charles asked cautiously.

"I never say what I don't mean. I'm really glad I agreed to take Tamera's place. And that's saying a lot, because I'd sworn to give up boys forever."

Charles eyes opened wide in surprise. "Why?"

"Because I'd decided all guys were jerks," Tia said. "My math teacher, Mr. Wilson, has been giving me a hard time. He doesn't believe that girls belong in honors math."

"That is so dumb," Charles said. "Why does he think that?"

"Because he thinks girls don't make use of their education."

"What century is he from?" Charles demanded. "My mom is a math teacher, and probably a better one than Mr. Wilson. Is there anything I can do to help?"

"You already did, Charles," Tia said, smiling up

at him. "You reminded me that most guys aren't like Mr. Wilson. Some guys are warm and sensitive and . . ."

"You want me to go beat him up for you?" Charles asked.

"You are too much," Tia said, laughing with him. "This is turning into a great evening."

"Hey, I love this song," Charles said. "Let's dance!" He took Tia's hand to lead her onto the floor.

Tamera's heart was going a mile a minute as she approached the lighted entrance to the auditorium. Please let him be there, she prayed. She was scared she had imagined the whole thing and Barry hadn't really asked her at all.

Then a figure stepped out of the shadows. "Hey, baby. You made it on time," Barry said. He was looking just as she had imagined—white tux, red bow tie, red silk vest over a pleated shirt. He was so gorgeous that she couldn't stop looking at him. She took off her coat and noticed that he was eyeing her with appreciation. "Nice dress," he said. "Looking good. Let's get in there and knock 'em dead, okay?"

He took her hand and led her in through the open doors. Tamera noticed heads turn. Couples stopped dancing to look at them. It was just like in her wildest dreams.

"I need to put my coat down somewhere," she said, looking around. "Do you see an empty table?"

The music changed to a loud hip-hop beat.

"My kind of music," Barry said, snapping his fingers. "Drop that coat and get out here, woman. I want to dance."

He threw down Tamera's coat and dragged her onto the dance floor. He was, as Tamera had imagined, a great dancer. She tried to copy his movements.

"What are you doing?" he demanded. "That's not how you do it. Don't you know anything?"

"Sorry," Tamera said. "I don't know these moves."

"I can see that. Do what I do. You're making me look bad."

Tamera swallowed hard. "Okay," she said. She chewed on her lip as she tried to follow Barry's complicated steps.

She was relieved when the music changed to a slow number with a deep, pulsing beat. Barry was still dancing a few feet away from her. Suddenly he looked across the room, then grabbed her and pulled her into his arms, holding her so tightly that she could hardly breathe.

"Tamera, baby," he whispered into her ear.

Tamera wondered what had made him change so quickly. Suddenly he was acting as if he really liked her. She wasn't complaining. Being held like this in Barry's arms was exactly what she had dreamed of. And yet now he was holding her close, she didn't feel the fireworks she had imagined. The scent of his aftershave was overpowering her, and she felt uneasy being held like this with everyone watching. She closed her eyes and hoped the magic would take over.

When Tamara opened her eyes again, she saw Whitney dancing close to them with another guy. The guy's arms were around Whitney, and she was gazing up at him adoringly. Immediately Barry took Tamera's face in his hands and kissed her.

She heard Whitney laugh. "Nice acting, Barry, but you're not fooling anybody," Whitney said.

"Better acting than you're doing," Barry said, pulling Tamera closer to him.

"I guess you must be pretty desperate, if you couldn't find anybody better than her," Whitney went on.

"There's nothing wrong with Tamera. She's cool and she does what I want, which is more than I can say for you."

"Are you still going on about that?" Whitney demanded. "You're still sore because I let Marcus give me a ride home?"

"I told you I was coming to pick you up."

"But you didn't, did you? I was waiting there in the rain and you didn't show up."

"So I was running late," Barry snapped. "You had no right to jump into another guy's car."

"I had every right. You don't own me, Barry Blackwell," Whitney yelled.

Tamera stood between them, feeling invisible.

"So you're saying you don't want to be my girl anymore, huh?" Barry demanded.

"I'm saying that if you really cared about me, you wouldn't leave me stranded on a dark street."

"I didn't do it on purpose," Barry said. "In fact I was coming to get you as fast as I could. It wasn't my fault that I got stopped by the cops for speeding and they took forever to write the ticket."

"You got stopped for speeding?" Whitney's voice faltered. "You never told me that."

"You never gave me a chance. You jumped into Marcus's car and let him drive you home."

"And you yelled at me for not waiting."

"I guess we were both kind of wrong," Barry said after a long pause.

"We each have a short fuse," Whitney agreed. "That's why we go together so well."

"Yeah," Barry said. "That must be it. I'm sorry I yelled at you, babe."

"I'm sorry I didn't wait for you, honey. It must have been real scary to be stopped by the police like that."

"And it must have been real scary to be out

there alone in the dark," Barry added. "Do you forgive me?"

"Sure I do. If you forgive me."

"No question," Barry said. His arms had slipped away from Tamera's waist. "I've missed you, babe," Barry said. "I hate it when you're not around."

Suddenly Barry and Whitney were in each other's arms. All Tamera could do was stand there, feeling totally embarrassed, in the middle of the dance floor. It was obvious they had forgotten she existed. She glanced around then slipped between the dancing couples to the side where Barry had dropped her coat on the floor. She picked it up, shook it out, and draped it around a chair. She found that her hands were shaking. How could she have been such an idiot to think that Barry had suddenly fallen in love with her. She realized now that he had only asked her to make Whitney mad. Now what was she going to do?

Then she remembered—she had another partner waiting for her, a partner who really wanted to be with her. She edged her way around the dance floor until she was standing where she could signal Tia. All she had to do was to get Tia out of the room for a second, then she could take her place. Tia wouldn't mind. She hadn't wanted to go to the dance in the first place. This was all going to work out just fine after all!

# Chapter 13

๏๏

*T*ia closed her eyes contentedly. The music had changed to a slow beat, and Charles slipped his arms around her waist. When Tia looked up at him and smiled, he drew her closer to him and she rested her head against his shoulder. Everything is working out just great, she thought. If Tamera hadn't gotten into another of her mix-ups, Tia would never have even come to the dance and she wouldn't have met Charles.

Tia opened her eyes and thought she saw someone waving at her from the darkness of the passageway outside. She looked again and noticed the sparkle of a silver dress. It had to be Tamera. She was waving like crazy. Something had to be wrong—maybe Ray had called to change their pick-up time, or maybe Tamera wanted to ride home with Barry instead.

"I'll be back in a second," Tia said, drawing away from Charles. "Don't go away, will you?"

"I'll go get us some punch," Charles said.

"Good plan," Tia said. "See you in a minute."

She ran over to Tamera. "Hi, what's up?" she said.

Tamera grabbed her and pulled her out of sight of the dance floor. "I came to say thanks, but I don't need you anymore," Tamera said. "I bet you're relieved, right?"

"What are you talking about?" Tia demanded.

"I don't need you to pretend to be me anymore," Tamera said. "I'm not with Barry anymore."

"What happened?"

"That creep," Tamera said. "I should have known, Tia. I thought it was to good to be true, and it was. He only invited me to make Whitney mad."

"Are you sure?"

"It was totally obvious. They had had a fight so she said she'd go to the dance with someone else, so he invited me to get back at her. They made up right in the middle of the dance floor."

"I see," Tia said slowly. "So now you don't have a partner."

"Sure I do," Tamera said. "Lucky I made two dates, for insurance, right?"

"No, Tamara," Tia said firmly. "Not right. It wasn't right what you did to Charles in the first place, and now he's having a great time with me."

"So? He can go on having a good time with the real me now," Tamera said. "I'll call my dad and ask him to come get you early."

"I'm not going home, Tamera," Tia said. "And I'm not giving up Charles."

Tamera's eyes opened wide in surprise.

"You asked me to dance with Charles, and that's what I'm doing," Tia said. "Too bad, Tamera, but I'm not giving him up."

"Don't tell me you actually like him?"

"I think he's great, if you want to know. I'm having the best time. We like all the same things."

"But you hate guys, remember?"

"So I was wrong, Tia said. "I've found out that some guys are really nice. Charles and I just hit it off right away."

"But he thinks you're me."

"Not anymore," Tia said.

"You told him?"

"He guessed—right after I said that science was my favorite subject."

"Tia! Why did you do a dumb thing like that?"

"Because I was enjoying talking to him so much that I forgot I was supposed to be you," Tia said.

"I was planning to tell him the truth, but he guessed anyway."

"So what are we going to do now?" Tamera asked. "He can't dance with both of us, and he asked *me* to the dance."

"And you begged me to take your place, remember?" Tia said. "You got us together, and now we really like each other. I'm sorry it didn't work out for you with Barry, but too bad."

"So what am I supposed to do now?" Tamera demanded. "I can't be at the dance without a partner."

"What about Whitney's partner?"

"I don't even know who he was. He just disappeared when Barry and Whitney got together."

"You can come and join Charles and me, I guess," Tia said. "You don't really need a partner for most dances, do you?"

"But I'd feel stupid," Tamera said. "Everyone will see that I don't have a partner."

"Allow me to take care of that, my little flower," said a voice in her ear.

Tamera spun around. Roger was standing there, looking taller and more mature than usual in a white tux with a red rose in his buttonhole.

"Roger!" Tamera exclaimed.

"The same guy who worships the ground you tread on," Roger said.

"What are you doing here?" Tamera demanded.

"I decided to show up, just in case you needed me," Roger said. "And it looks like you do need me. Now you and I can boogie our way to the stars. Prepare yourself for a night to remember, honeybun."

"How could I ever forget it?" Tamera asked, with a despairing glance to Tia as Roger whisked he onto the dance floor.

"I've learned my lesson," Tamera said to Tia as she flopped onto her bed later that night.

"That you're never going to make dates with two guys again?"

"That, too," Tamera said. "But I meant that I'm never going to fall for a guy just because of the way he looks. Barry was really a jerk, Tia. Whitney might like being bossed around like that, but I don't. No guy is ever going to snap his fingers and expect me to come running."

"Way to go, sister," Tia said, smiling.

"In fact I'll be happy to join your protest marches as long as you need me. We need to get the message out that guys have no reason to think they're so hot."

"I'm not going to be doing any more pro-testing," Tia said. "We have a meeting set up with the principal on Monday. He's promised to take care of our problem. And anyway, I've learned my lesson, too. I've learned that there are good guys and bad guys. Charles, for example . . ."

"Oh, please." Tamera sighed. "You've done nothing but talk about Charles all night. He's a nice guy but nothing special."

"I think he's very special," Tia said. "He likes all the things I like. We laughed at the same things tonight. We like the same music. He's a great dancer, and he has the cutest smile, too. It's perfect."

"Different strokes for different folks," Tamera said, rolling her eyes. "I never imagined that my helpful geek was someone else's hunk."

"I guess that's what's nice about life," Tia said. "We don't all fall in love with the same person."

Tamera nodded. "Lucky for us that we just look alike. Imagine if we fought over the same boys all the time!"

Tia laughed. "We'd have killed each other by now," she said.

"It's funny that we're so alike in some ways and so different in others," Tamera said thoughtfully.

Tia lay back on her pillow. "That's what makes it such fun being us," she said. "I never quite know what crazy thing my twin sister is going to do next."

"Speak for yourself," Tamera said. "I've never done a crazy thing in my life."

"Oh no? Only making two dates for the dance tonight! That was very smart."

"It was. Now I've found out that I wouldn't want Barry as a boyfriend, even if I could have him, and I wouldn't want Charles either, or I would be jealous of you right now. Just a smart way of figuring things out."

"Shut up!" Tia said, and laughed as she threw her pillow at Tamera.

On Monday morning Tia and the other girls in Mr. Wilson's math class met with Principal Vernon.

"I do understand that you girls have been having problems," he said. "And I want you to know that the school takes your problems very seriously. We want for our girls to succeed just as much as our boys."

Joanie glanced across at Tia and made a thumbs-up sign.

"It has been obvious to us in the administration for some time that Mr. Wilson isn't the ideal teacher for girls," Principal Vernon went on.

"So you're getting rid of him finally?" Wendy asked.

"That wouldn't be wise. Mr. Wilson has tenure here and he's an otherwise outstanding math teacher," Principal Vernon said. "What we've decided is to offer a separate honors class for girls this year. It's unusual to offer a class for just seven students, but we feel it's the right thing to do. Ms. Morgenstern will teach it."

Tia gave Joanie a puzzled look. She noticed that the other girls looked puzzled, too.

Tia cleared her throat. "Excuse me, Mr. Vernon, but I don't think this is what we want at all."

"I don't understand, Ms. Landry. Isn't this what you were protesting about?"

"We were protesting about being treated differently," Tia said. "And this is just showing the world that we are different. You're saying we don't belong in the regular honors class so you're going to make a special class for us. That's not right."

"I agree with Tia, Principal Vernon," Joanie added. "You're treating us like outcasts to give us our own class, separate from the boys."

Principal Vernon looked confused. "Then what do you want?"

"We want to feel that we're welcome in any class that we're qualified for," Tia said as Wendy and the others nodded in approval. "Even if that is auto shop or advanced physics."

The principal shrugged. "I've made you what I thought was a good offer, Ms. Landry. If you don't choose to take it, your alternatives are to go back to your old math class or to stay with Mr. Wilson."

"Then I guess I'll stay with Mr. Wilson," Tia said.

"Me, too," Joanie agreed.

"Maybe we can reprogram him to think girls are human beings," Wendy said, making them all laugh.

The principal was still shaking his head as they walked out of his office.

"You do think we're doing the right thing, don't you?" Joanie said to Tia as they walked down the hall.

"Of course we are. Splitting students into separate groups can only cause trouble. It never works."

"It would just make us feel like outsiders," Wendy said.

"So we're stuck with Mr. Wilson, huh?" Renee asked.

"If we quit his class, then he's won, hasn't he?" Tia said. "I say we stick it out and we protest loudly every time he puts one of us down. Maybe we'll pressure him so much that he'll decide to quit!"

They linked arms as they went into math together.

Mr. Wilson looked up in surprise to see them. "I understood you young ladies wouldn't be coming back," he said.

"Oh no, Mr. Wilson. We like it here," Wendy said sweetly. Tia suppressed a giggle as she went to her seat.

"We were just in the middle of choosing our mathlete team to compete against St. Joe's," Mr. Wilson said. "Any nominations?"

Jonathan, the boy next to Tia, raised his hand. "I nominate Tia Landry," he said.

Another hand was raised. "I nominate Wendy Rosenthal."

Then a voice from the back of the room called, "I nominate Joanie Chen."

Mr. Wilson's face turned red and then purple. "Is this some kind of joke, guys?"

"No, sir," Jonathan said. "You asked us to choose three people we wanted to represent us, and we chose the three best math students."

Mr. Wilson looked around the classroom. "Any more nominations? Ramon? What about you? How about Peter?"

There was silence.

"You really want three girls to represent you?" Mr. Wilson said in disbelief.

Jonathan got to his feet again. "We don't care," he said. "We think they could win the math contest for our school."

"All those in favor of these three representing our class," Mr. Wilson said, "please raise your hands."

Hands went up all over the classroom.

Tia was still in a daze when the bell rang. "Thanks for what you did, Jonathan," she said as she passed his seat. "We thought that you guys felt the same way as Mr. Wilson."

"Are you serious?' Marcus exclaimed. "That guy is a major pain. We were all totally embarrassed about the way he was treating you, but we couldn't think of what to do about it until now." He grinned at Tia. "Besides, I might need someone to whisper me the answers when he gives pop quizzes."

Tia was still smiling as she headed for her locker. It felt great to know that she had fought for what she believed in, and that she had won. It felt great to know that the boys in her class thought she was smart, and it felt extra great to know that Charles was waiting for her.

She started to run. She couldn't wait to tell Tamera!

## About the Author

Janet Quin-Harkin has written over fifty books for teenagers, including the best-seller *Ten-Boy Summer*. She is the author of several popular series: TGIF!, Friends, Heartbreak Café, Senior Year, and The Boyfriend Club. She has also written several romances.

Ms. Quin-Harkin lives with her husband in San Rafael, California. She has four children. In addition to writing books, she teaches creative writing at a nearby college.